PLAYING HEARTS

W.R. GINGELL

With many thanks to Lewis Carroll, whose Alice inspired—and continues to inspire—me.

1

———

It started the way it usually starts: with a card. It was on my pillow that morning when I woke, its red pips showing up clearly against the whiteness of the pillow-slip. The Jack of Hearts. I knew exactly who'd left it, and what would be on the back of it; but I turned it over anyway. It had been such a long time since I'd seen one. It said: *You're invited. It's a very important date. Don't be late.*

Only if I'm honest, that's probably not really where it started. Underland: that's where it started. Underland. Once you know, it's like leaping worlds every time you step over a puddle. In a way, it *is* leaping worlds. It's not just puddles, either: Alice got in through a looking-glass, and I've heard of a boy who gets in through windows. I've always liked puddles, though. Splashy and bright and exciting—and at first that's how Underland seems. It feels like anything is possible. Mind you, Underland is only my name for it. Other people know it by other names: Mirror World, Wonderland, Looking Glass World. It's all the same in the end. The same Underland. A whole, upside down world under the puddles.

I

2

———————

I don't remember much about my first journey to Underland. I was three at the time, and until I was seven, I was convinced it was all a dream. I was by myself in the hedge, hiding from the other children because it was there and I could, and because it was fun to watch people passing the foster home in which I lived. They never saw me.

But this time, someone did. I was curled up on one of the branches, my bare feet scratched and brown, and the first I knew was an eye looking at me through a gap in the hedge.

"You're invited," said the eye. It blinked, then disappeared. In its place a hand appeared, a card between its forefinger and middle finger. I took it without understanding what it was or what the voice meant by what it said. "It's a very important date. Don't be late."

I put the card in my already bulging pockets and forgot about it during the afternoon. And later I was too busy with milk and biscuits and getting out of brushing my teeth in the rush before bed to remember the card crumpled in my pocket.

That night, *she* sent the card sharks after me. I didn't know that's what they were—well, I didn't even know who *she* was. Not then. Midnight woke me, all silver and cool and snowy, and they were already by my bed, one on either side. Thin—no, *flat*— figures, inky black against the off-white walls, their flat, heavy feet shuffling against the carpet. They didn't speak; they simply made a soft *click-click* of noise. I found out later that this was their sharp teeth snapping open and shut.

"You're not allowed in here," I said, my voice very quiet against the clicking of pointed teeth. Mrs. Mack, my foster mother, was clear about men and bedrooms. If there was a man in the bedroom, I was supposed to scream. I wasn't sure why, but I knew it was Very Important. If it came to that, I wasn't exactly certain these *were* men, but I wanted them to know that I Wasn't Afraid. I was stubbornly Not Afraid when they clicked their teeth at me without speaking and threw a velvet sack over my head. I yelled and fought, but the velvet muffled my cries, and when at last the sack was thrown down on something hard and cold, they left me to fight my own way out of it. I emerged, ruffled and panting, in an icily cold room that seemed to stretch vastly around and above me. My green socks showed up vibrantly against the white marble tile I stood on, and as I clutched the velvet sack about my shoulders for warmth, I saw a confusion of angles in red and white all around me. There were too many corners and too many people. The confusion of angles bewildered my young mind, and I didn't realise I was in a vast hall of mirrors until I saw that all of the people were *me*.

No; not quite all of them. One set of them was taller than the set of reflections that was me. There was a boy standing next to me, watching with a kind of narrow-eyed curiosity as I gazed around me and finally grasped his presence. He was dressed in red velvet and gold lace, a thin, pale boy with a sharp, aristo- cratic nose and a pale gold fringe of hair swept to one side. He looked me up and down, lingering curiously on my bright green socks, and arched one light gold brow.

He said: "You're a funny looking little thing."

I gave him a perplexed glance but found it easier to look at him than the confusion of reflections. "I'm hungry," I said.

"Have some tarts," he said, offering me a tray. I wasn't sure where it had come from, but I had seen magicians on television before, after all.

"I'm not allowed," I said. That was another of Mrs. Mack's rules. No sweet things between meals. "Why are you awake? You should be in bed."

"*That's* no fun!" he said scornfully. "Why are you so small, little girl? I thought you'd be bigger."

"I'm only three," I said. I felt slightly resentful. I couldn't help being so small.

The boy made an unconvinced noise. "I suppose there must be something to you, if she chose you. We're to be engaged. Do you understand that?"

I only blinked at him. I had no idea what he meant, but I did know that the boy's lofty tones were annoying.

"Are you afraid of needles?"

"I've had my measles shot," I said, but I felt my lip tremble. I very much disliked needles.

"It's all right," he said, with a sigh. "I'll hold your hand. You're not to cry."

"I don't cry," I told him, but I let him take my hand anyway.

He said coolly: "I'm Jack. They didn't tell me your name."

"I'm Mabel. What—who were those men? They put me in a sack."

"They're not men," said Jack. He was just a little paler, and his voice had dropped to a whisper. "They're card sharks. Stay away from them. They bite."

I opened my mouth to say that men didn't bite, but the concentric reflections of myself were doing something interesting behind Jack's back. They grew: or maybe I grew. I wasn't sure. Soon my reflection was tall and quite grown up, with long hair and a wasp-waisted red gown. Beside it a single drop of red appeared in the mirror and grew rapidly. Jack looked over his shoulder and went a little paler, which interested me. I didn't know it was possible for a boy to be that white. He turned his eyes back on the drop, which was now about the size of an armchair and had begun to look a little like a woman in a very big dress if I looked at it the right way.

Jack's fingers pinched mine. "Don't speak to her," he said in a whisper. "Just nod. And don't look her in the eyes. She doesn't like that. Hold out your hand when she asks for it, and don't cry."

"I don't cry," I said again. Between his warning and the way the red blot was growing, I somehow wasn't very surprised to see a woman eventually standing before us, her crimson skirts embroidered with jet and rubies in the shape of hearts, and a small, silver mirror hanging from a beautiful silver belt by the side of her bodice's point. I didn't dare to look any higher than that because Jack had become entirely silent, his back very straight and stiff. Still, I had the impression that this woman was wearing a sharp, vastly tall golden crown. Since the only person I knew with a crown was the Queen of England, it seemed obvious that this must be she. I would have asked her if she was, but I could feel Jack's fingers curled around mine, warm and tight, and remembered that I wasn't supposed to speak. I fixed my eyes on her belt buckle instead, and gripped Jack's velvet sleeve with my free hand.

"Hah!" said a voice as sharp as the crown. It came from somewhere behind us, and Jack and I spun together to find her standing there at our backs, trapping us between herself and her reflection. "Here it is at last! No, turn back around, you stupid child!"

I was inclined to be sulky, but Jack turned me back around

with him, and I felt fingers grip my shoulders, red polish flashing in my peripheral. The Queen smelled of cold and roses. One of her hands left my shoulder to tilt up my chin, and I found myself gazing at a reflection that held only myself. It was the big version of myself that I'd seen earlier. I didn't much like it, because my face was pinched and narrow, and not very nice.

"Very good!" purred the Queen, releasing me, and the reflection went back to showing what it should have shown. Only it wasn't *quite* right, because the reflection of the mirror hanging from the Queen's belt showed something else. There was bigger me again; only I was in a green dress, with my hair tumbled around me and glass flying.

"Oh!" I said, my eyes wide.

"Don't gape!" snapped the Queen, shocking me out of the sight. "Turn around, pinch-face!"

Jack and I turned once more, our hands still clasped, and this time when I saw the mirror at the Queen's belt, it showed nothing but real reflections. She said impatiently: "Give me your hand, child!"

I did as I was told, my gaze still on the silver mirror that showed things that weren't in the room, and something sharp pierced my finger. I instinctively tried to pull my hand away, but her fingers pinched harder than Jack's, cruel and strong. I saw a huge drop of blood well up on the tip of my finger, as richly velvet as the queen's frock. Beside me, Jack offered one narrow, white hand without being told. I looked up once through my lashes, and saw the exulting, cruel smile on the queen's lips as she pricked his finger too. Jack took it without a sound and reached for my bloodied hand with his own, but the Queen's smile made me feel odd and squishy in a way that the meeting of our bloodied hands didn't.

"Done!" said the queen, in her harsh voice. "Bound by blood, in life as in death. Take your fiancée out to the garden, Jack: her thin little face irritates me. Send her back home when you've finished playing with her." There was a heavy swirl of velvet and she vanished in a glitter of reflective glass.

The tickle of something wet dripping down my injured hand reminded me of my wrongs, and I let go of Jack's hand to study it. Now that the worst of the pain was over it was interesting to watch the trickles of blood as they made crimson channels down my hand.

"Come along," said Jack, tugging me out of contemplation by my uninjured hand. I was towed toward what at first seemed to be a pair of mirrors but eventually proved to be mirror-lined doors, outlined in impossible golden sunshine. Both of the doors had an elegant red-lacquered doorknob, but Jack didn't touch them. Instead, he pushed them open with his injured hand, very deliberately leaving a bloody handprint on the glass.

"She won't like it," he said, when he saw me looking at it; "But it's not against the rules, so she can't do anything about it."

I found myself walking out into a garden that was bathed in bright sunshine, my green socks picking up late autumn leaves as I trailed after Jack in the grass. "Why is the sun out? It's night."

"Mother made him come out. He didn't want to, but she's queen after all."

"Where's the moon, then?"

"She's up there too, but she's sulking. She doesn't like it when the sun comes out during the night. She's a feminist and she doesn't believe in being eclipsed by a male. Sit down here."

Here was the brick side of a fountain. I did as I was told and Jack sat down beside me, scooping water in his gory hand. "Sorry about the blood," he said. He washed my hand quickly and competently: I got the impression, young as I was, that he'd had to wash away blood many times before. "She likes the old rituals. It'll heal quickly."

"Why did she prick me with a needle?"

"Do you only ever ask questions?"

I gazed at him silently until he gave a small sniff of laughter.

"It's meant to bind us together. It's all very old-fashioned and pointless, and it amounts to the fact that we're to be married."

"I'm too young to marry," I said. "And I don't have a nice dress."

Jack rinsed his own hand carelessly and flicked bloody drops of water on the grass. I didn't understand the look in his eyes, but his voice sounded rather harsh when he said: "We won't be married until I'm twenty-five. That's sixteen years to buy nice clothes. Or to do an awful lot of running."

I don't remember much else from that day. I remember Jack pointing out a sharp red building that rose from a sprawl of other buildings on the horizon—the Heart Castle, he called it— and telling me that we were outside the Queen's Mirror Hall; but I must have fallen asleep at some stage, there in the sunlit night. When I woke the next day I found myself lying on top of all the bedcovers, my finger still sore. The tiny scar vanished in a day or two, and as young as I was, it wasn't long before I came to believe that I had dreamed it all. But every now and then I was certain that I caught sight of a flash of red in my dressing table mirror, and once the pair of black-flecked eyes I saw gazing back at me from a window at preschool were not my own.

3

I accidentally went back into Underland the year I turned seven. It was one of those hot, muggy summer days that crawl in under your collar and wriggle uncomfortably down your back. Not a breath of wind; and the pond in the park was so clear and reflective that I could see everything around me in its waters. I jumped in with both feet and a joyful splash, and slipped through into Underland almost before I was aware of it.

This time I came out in a teapot, with my eyes wide open. It was a very big teapot, but it was still an odd place to come out. Someone said: "Dormy! Is that you?" and peered at me with dilated pupils that were deep purple, the teapot lid held aloft in one big hand.

"My name is Mabel," I told him.

"Mind your elbows, then."

"WHO IS IT?" demanded another voice. I looked across the table and found a large grey hare staring fixedly at me. There was a hard, speculative look to its eyes.

"IT'S A MABEL!" bawled the other, despite the fact that the hare could see me quite well for itself.

"WELL, TELL IT TO KEEP ITS ELBOWS TO ITSELF!"

"My elbows are still in the teapot," I told them both.

"Oh," said the purple-eyed man, putting the teapot lid down on the tablecloth. He was a tall, gangly thing with big hands and feet, and a syncopated blink that almost amounted to a nervous twitch. A curving, oddly-proportioned top-hat with a curling brim sat sideways on his spiky hair. "Mind you don't block the spout, then."

"Actually, I was going to climb out," I said.

The purple-eyed man gave me a fascinated look. "Were you, though? How do you manage that without legs?"

"I have legs!"

"WHAT'S THAT IT SAYS?"

"IT SAYS IT HAS LEGS!"

"YES, BUT HOW DO WE KNOW? WERE WE GIVEN A VOTE?"

"*I* wasn't," I said, jumping myself up on the teapot rim. "I just got them. I don't see why you should have had a vote."

"WHY IS IT DOING THAT?"

The purple-eyed man bawled: "I THINK IT'S TRYING TO CLIMB OUT!"

"HOW DOES IT MANAGE WITHOUT LEGS?"

"*I have legs!*" I yelled. The hare fixed its gaze upon me again just as I worked one leg out of the teapot. I waggled my foot at it.

"What do you know," said the hare, in a much more moderate voice. "It has a leg. How fortunate for it! I wish I had a leg."

"You do," I said. "You have two."

"Two is different than one," said the hare sternly. "You should be more precise, small child."

"I have two legs as well," I said, in order to be more precise.

"As well as *what*, exactly?"

I paused to think it through carefully. "Well, two arms, I suppose."

They both stared at me for a long moment. At length, in a much friendlier voice, the purple-eyed man said: "So you have."

I smiled cautiously at him and looked around me with fascinated eyes. My teapot was perched on a long, narrow table that followed the verdant swell of a grassy hill and vanished over the summit. Behind me was a forest with grass of a very different green to that beneath the table, and when I looked back toward the summit of the hill, I thought I saw a sharp, red building far away on the horizon. I shivered at the sight of it. I'd had nightmares about something like that, I was sure; when I was very young. I looked away from it and back at the tea-laden table. It was shadowed by trees and dappled with sunlight, and the sunlight was oddly familiar, too.

"I think I've been here before," I said, slowly.

"You can't have been," said the purple-eyed man. "I would have noticed. So would Dormy. He usually sleeps in there."

I sat down on the colourful, patched tablecloth and frowningly considered the world around me. "The sun is all wrong."

"Sssshh!" hissed the Hare. "He'll hear you! We've only just got him to stop sulking about the summer storms."

"And the moon is a lady," I said slowly, with a growing sense of *deja vu*.

"Well, I wouldn't go so far as to say *that*," said the purple-eyed man. "She's *female*."

"Is it day or night?"

Perhaps the question annoyed them: the Hare immediately went back to his deafening bellow.

"WHAT'S SHE ASKING?"

"SHE WANTS TO KNOW IF IT'S DAY OR NIGHT!"

"IS SHE AN IMBECILE?"

"I *know* the sun is out," I said crossly. "But last time I was here he was out at night."

That made one pair of purple eyes flicker madly around my face in a series of rag-time blinks, and one pair of black ones narrow intensely at me. "We don't know any knights," said the Hare more calmly. "Nasty people, knights. The Queen owns all of them."

"I didn't meet you last time," I said, ignoring that remark as incomprehensible. "Who are you?"

"Alive," said the purple-eyed man.

"Moderately healthy," said the Hare.

"Happy–"

"Moderately–"

"*Who* are you, not *how* are you," I said. I flicked a look between the two of them and said testingly, "That was stretching a bit."

Purple eyes slid sideways and back. Black eyes regarded me slyly. "Her ears are bigger than Dormy's ears," said the Hare.

"I did notice," said the other. To me, he said: "I'm the Hatter. You may have noticed."

"Noticed? Oh, the hat. Yes. It's very...*odd*."

"Thank you!" said the Hatter simply. "I made it 'specially! Do you know what skill and dexterity it takes to make a hat with this kind of oddity? Facets from every realm of probability and even a few from the realms of possibility!"

I didn't understand that, but from my position atop the tea-table I could see a coach fast approaching over the crown of the hill, so I asked instead, "Who's that? In that old-fashioned coach? Are those horses?"

"Horses are for courses, not for coaches," said the Hare disapprovingly. "Those are card sharks."

I had a brief, unsettling memory—or was it a dream?—of

sharp teeth clicking at me, and the red velvet darkness of a sack that I seemed to remember being thrown over me. "I've *been* here before," I said again, with a squeak in my voice.

"Back! Back in the teapot!" said the Hatter frantically, poking me in the stomach with his long fingers in an attempt to overbalance me back into the teapot. "Mind your ears, back in the pot!"

I fended off his fingers and darted behind an oversized milk jug. "Ow! Stop it!"

"SHE WASN'T INVITED," said the Hare. I thought he meant me, but he was looking at the coach with wide, wild eyes. I understood why as soon as a card shark sprang from the back of the coach and opened the door. The first thing to emerge from the coach was a vast balloon of red velvet punctured by a small, silver mirror, and one pointed red shoe. The balloon grew in size until it was dimpled by a bodice in white lace that had a front point as sharp as the shoe, then the Queen's terrifyingly straight back descended in a line exactly parallel to the slanted steps. It had been four years since I'd seen her—four years of the real world being ground into me by life in a series of foster homes—but it hadn't been quite long enough to purge the deeply buried nightmare memory of her. I was old enough this time to know that she wasn't the Queen of England, though I was still certain she was a Queen. She wasn't wearing a crown this time, but her head-dress was so wide that it almost overtook her skirt in size. A cloud of white netting adorned it and frothed behind her as she at last extricated herself from the coach: it was the last of her ensemble to emerge from the door.

The Hatter, his big hands white-knuckled around his tea-cup, mumbled to himself: "Wasn't invited. No room. No room at all. Wasn't invited and shouldn't be offered tea."

The card shark closed the coach door and put up the stairs again, but the coach wasn't quite empty. Through the window I could see a head of pale golden hair, slicked back and smooth, above a collar of dark crimson. It turned slightly to the side, displaying an arrogantly tilted chin and a narrow, aristocratic nose, and I felt the clutch of my fingers in the fabric at my waist. My finger—the one that had been pricked in that odd, childish dream so many years ago—was hurting.

"Jack," I said, the name falling rusty with disuse from my lips.

"What did I tell you?" whispered the Hare, frantically soft. "Her ears are *huge!*"

As the Queen shook her skirts out in massive stateliness, I dropped from the table to the grass, scuttling between chair legs and tablecloth until I was safe beneath the table. There were grass-stains on my clothes but I ignored them, wriggling vigorously until I could see a sliver of the action from beneath the scalloped edge of tablecloth. The Hatter's legs were close, and I hugged his skinny ankles, pressing my cheek to the purple stockings and tattooing the buckle from his knee-breeches on my left temple. It was by far the least comfortable position I'd ever been in, but I wouldn't have traded it for the most comfortable seat at the tea table. Not when the Queen was sweeping toward it with fear before her and danger in her wake. Behind her the coach window framed Jack, who didn't move—who didn't even look toward the unfortunate two at the tea-table. Almost as if he knew that things were about to become unpleasant for Hatter and Hare. Why was the Queen so angry?

"I see you're still at tea," she said. The card sharks had ranged behind her in something like a v-formation, but as she drew closer to the table they spread out to surround us. Three of them mounted chairs and then the table to cross over to the Hare's side. I heard their sharp, metallic footsteps on the table above my head, and then the soft thunk of feet hitting grass behind me. I didn't like them being out of my sight, but I preferred to keep my eyes on the Queen.

"I like to think that I'm not a demanding monarch," she was saying pleasantly. "However, I really do expect my subjects to rise when I deign to approach them. Remove your hat, man!"

I let go of the Hatter's ankles just in time. He scrambled to his feet, and the billowing of the tablecloth suggested that he was bowing.

Across the table, the Hare's voice said: "WHAT'S THAT SHE SAYS? SHE WANTS TO REVIEW THE CAT?" and was cut off in a grunt as something metallic went *schwik!* There was a thump on the table-top—was the Hare dead? I felt my lower lip tremble, and heard Jack's younger voice saying again: *You're not to cry.*

I wasn't crying. I *wasn't.*

Above my head, the Queen's voice said: "I'd hate to think that you're sharing your...*tea*...around Underland. It's not healthy."

There was a garbled mumble from the Hare that made me thankfully aware that he was still alive, and Hatter sat down. I immediately seized his legs again, and though they were as skinny as ever they weren't as stiff. I had the feeling he was as glad for me as I was for him.

"Not healthy for you, and certainly not healthy for them," said the Queen. I didn't think she was really talking about tea, but for the life of me I couldn't figure out what she *was* talking about. "The type of tea you're spreading about has a nasty habit of poisoning the drinkers."

"Poisoned tea is no use," said Hatter, his legs quivering. "All our guests would die. Dead guests are *so hard* to entertain. Perhaps a little sip of Syrup of Poppies instead?"

"Number Six, restrain the Hare," said the Queen. Her voice was soft and plump, like a pillow. A pillow pressed against my face so that I couldn't breathe. "I've heard that a hare's foot is good luck."

Above my head there was a brief, violent struggle, the sound of smashing crockery and what sounded like the Hare's huge back feet beating against the tabletop.

"CALUMNY!" yelled the Hare, his voice more frenzied than before. "A HARE MAKES HIS OWN LUCK, MADAM!"

"Or is it a rabbit's foot for luck?" wondered the Queen. "Perhaps it was a hare's foot for face powder. Do you know, I'm almost certain that it *is*. Oh, hold him down Number Six! I don't care *where* you're bleeding."

"NEVER TOUCHED A GRAIN OF POWDER IN MY LIFE!" bawled the Hare. "LIES! ALL LIES!"

I gripped Hatter's knocking knees harder, my confused brain trying to make sense of the Queen's subtleties and the Hare's babble. They were doing an even more incomprehensible version of the adult talk I heard at my ever-changing foster homes. I wriggled myself down until I was clutching Hatter's ankles instead of his knees, and carefully peeked out beneath the hem of the tablecloth again. My eyes travelled up her red pouf of a dress until I was staring unblinkingly at her right ear. I didn't quite dare to look at her face properly: part of me still remembered a time when Jack had warned me against looking her in the eye, and I seemed to remember a nightmare smile I'd once glimpsed.

Jack. What was Jack doing? Why was he in the coach? Why wasn't he helping poor Hatter and Hare? I wriggled out a little further, the tablecloth draping around my head, and craned my head to look around the Queen's skirt at the coach. Jack was still there, gazing out on the scene. His eyes were inattentive and even slightly bored, his upper lip curled. He was playing with a ring that was big enough to see from where I was. I considered waving at him, but I was too frightened of the

Queen to try it. Besides, how was I to know if he would be willing to help? He certainly wasn't doing anything at the moment. I glared at him from my hiding place, and as if he felt my eyes on him, I saw Jack's eyes rise from his ring, slowly, slowly; panning from ring to window, then to grass, and from grass to–

Me. He saw me.

His eyes widened slightly, his fingers curling suddenly over the scrollwork at the window. I gripped the Hatter's legs a little tighter: was Jack going to call out to his mother? The Hatter's hand, trembling slightly, appeared below the tablecloth and passed me a small, iced cake. I took it in my own damp hand and insensibly squashed it almost to dough, my eyes flying to the coach and Jack's face again. His index finger was up, and as I watched he lowered his finger slowly with his eyes steadily on me. *Get back under the tablecloth*, said the gesture. I wriggled back a little way but kept to my position despite Jack's narrowed eyes. All of him was narrower—older and narrower—and I didn't think he looked as nice as he had looked when he was younger. It seemed like he was still watching out for me, though, and that made me feel better. Why wasn't he watching out for Hatter and Hare as well?

And *what* was the Hatter saying? "Really weren't expecting you," I heard him reiterate sullenly. "No room. Absolutely no room."

Even to my seven-year-old brain, that stuck out. They had both said it: Hatter and Hare. *Weren't expecting. No room. Not invited.* And so loudly. Almost...almost as if they *hoped* to be overheard. But overheard by whom?

"Don't lose your heads," said the Queen pleasantly. "I've no interest in your poxy little tea party. The only interest I have is making sure that you don't import it to any other tea-tables."

"Don't import tea," said the Hatter. "All Underland leaf,

purple as it comes. Import biscuits sometimes. Danish butter cookies."

"Then I suppose our interview is at an end. Before I go, however, I'd like to leave you both a little reminder. Number Five, cut off the Hare's forepaw."

A scream, shrill and inhuman, jolted me with such force that I jerked away from Hatter's legs, instinctively curling in a ball with my quivering arms wrapped around my knees. There was a kind of fizzing in my ears, and my eyes, frozen open in shock, saw the blossoming of wet redness on the Hare's side of the tablecloth.

"Oh, I'm sorry," said the Queen, her voice softer than ever. It was hard to hear through the buzzing in my ears. "Did I say *leave*? I meant *take*. Bring it with you, Number Five."

I heard the massive rustling of her skirts as she swept away, heard the slap of the card sharks' feet over the tabletop to follow her; but all I could understand was the spreading patch of red with its liquid centre and quickly browning edges. The coach must have rolled away again at some stage. I didn't notice; but somewhere in all the whimpering and blood and moaning, Hatter's big hands pulled me from beneath the table. When I came back to myself, shivering away my shock, I was curled up on a large, spotted dinner plate with Hatter patting my head as if I was a small dog instead of a small girl. Through the tears in my eyes I could see a blurry grey and red figure across the table.

"Blue blood!" whimpered the Hare. "Father told me I was blue blood. Hatter, they took my blue blood and pumped me full of red. I'll never be royalty now."

"Tea and cake," said Hatter, with terrifying calmness. "You'll be as good as new."

That made me sit up, because I was very sure that tea and cake were not going to help something that was bleeding as freely as the Hare's stub of an arm was bleeding. "You have to sew him up," I said, pushing my tears away with the grass-stained heel of my palm. "He'll die, otherwise."

"*Tea* and *cake*," Hatter said obstinately. He reached over me to the sausage warmer, and when he lifted the lid I found that it wasn't a sausage warmer but an iron stove-top. Where was the rest of it? It certainly hadn't been under the table when I hid beneath it: I would have noticed that scorching heat.

"Back in the teapot," the Hatter said, and suited the action to the words by lifting me by the collar and depositing me gently inside. He put the lid back on it, but cracked it open again for a brief moment to add: "And don't pop your top."

I found myself sitting in the herby dregs of cold tea, and shivered. Was he trying to send me back? I didn't think it worked that way. Outside my teapot someone screamed again, sharp and short, and I hit my head on the teapot lid with a clang. Perhaps that's what Hatter meant by telling me not to pop my top. Regardless of the warning, I shoved myself up and out of the teapot, my eyes blinking against the sudden return of brightness.

"Hare?" I said, in a tremulous voice. "Are you all right?"

"Nice little girls don't sit in the tea," said Hare, his voice a rasp. He was still there across the table, his eyes blacker and wilder than before, but his mutilated arm was behind his back and there was a singed sort of smell to the air. One of them had haphazardly piled teacups and saucers over the sticky red stain on the tablecloth; and the sausage warmer, which seemed to exude the singed smell most strongly, now had a cake perched on its lid.

"Nice little girls stay in the teapot when they're put there," added Hatter reproachfully.

There didn't seem to be anything sensible to say to such contradictory statements, so I merely said: "The tea was cold anyway," and climbed back out.

Hare made a fastidious *moue*. "Ugh. Cold tea."

"If you ask the sun nicely, he'll dry you out," said Hatter.

"Oh. Won't he do that anyway?"

"Yes, but this way he won't sulk about it."

I was almost certain that Hatter was changing the subject, but I was feeling rather chilly, so I merely held my damp skirt away from my underwear and said to the warm sky: "Please will you dry my skirt?"

The sun became noticeably warmer, a radiant, personal presence that dried the wet tea in no time and somehow managed to warm the inner chilled feeling that had nothing to do with the cold tea. As my skirt dried and stained slightly, I said to Hare: "How is your hand?"

"Wouldn't know," said Hare, shifting the stub a little further behind his back. "*She's* got it. She could be mistreating it, for all I know. Didn't even get a chance to say goodbye."

I left my skirt to its own mending in the sunshine and leaned over to kiss Hare's wiry cheek by way of consolation. "That's not a medically proven remedy," said Hare, but he seemed pleased and the wildness in his eyes faded a little.

"Why is the Queen so angry with you both?"

"She's jealous of my hat," sighed Hatter.

I looked up at it, then back at Hatter. "She has a crown. Why would she want your hat?"

"Can you see the past, present and future in a crown? Of course not! All you see in a crown is a reflection of yourself."

"What do you see in your hat, then?" I asked curiously.

"Your ears are still too big," said Hatter. "You should do something about that. Think of Underland as a pool. No, think of it as a looking-glass—no! as a reflection."

"Why?"

"Well, Underland isn't real. Well, it is, but it's a different real to everyone: it depends on how you see things. You come by water, but it's contrariwise to those who come by looking-glass. We're a different reflection."

"Oh," I said thoughtfully. I thought I might have the smallest inkling of what Hatter was talking about. His top hat was sewn with myriad shiny pieces of reflective material: a bunch of oddly-shimmering sequins here, a piece of mirror-like satin there. There were even chips of glass in the tall, curving height of it, and I was certain that the patch at the top was a small, rippling piece of water. Did Hatter see Underland contrariwise, too?

"You can see a different reflection of Underland in your hat," I said. I had an idea that was beyond my understanding to grasp, and without being capable of voicing it, I finished lamely: "It's *different*."

"It's time for you to go home," Hatter said abruptly.

A little indignantly, I demanded: "What did *I* do?"

"What *will* you do?" countered Hatter, and swept me from the table in a flutter of tea-stained skirt. "Don't think I've haven't seen the ripples *you* make in the reflections!"

"I don't make ripples," I said in confusion, as Hatter dragged me away across the grass and toward an ornamental pool.

"DID SO TOO!" hollered Hare, back at the table. "JUMPED RIGHT IN, DIDN'T YOU? BOTH FEET!"

"Yes, but that was because I was jumping into water!"

"Exactly," said Hatter, hefting me up onto the pool's rim. "What did I tell you? And ripples make things hard to see."

"Will I be coming back?" I asked, anxious to stay. I was afraid for Hatter and Hare.

"Shouldn't think we can stop you," said Hatter, and pushed me off the rim.

I made a tiny, off-balanced bunny hop into the water. For a breathless moment I both felt the splash of it around my ankles and the weight of it rushing over my head in waves of pressure.

Hatter's anxious purple eyes followed me through the rippling of water. I thought I could still see him when the splashing of water around my ankles died away into ripples and I found myself ankle-deep in the pond in the real world. I knew I was back in Australia because the sun here wasn't anywhere near as personal as Underland's sun. It was just warm, muggy, Australian summer.

4
———

I told myself that I would be better prepared next time I found myself in Underland. I never really felt that I'd quite gone away, if it came to that: the feeling of being watched that I'd had ever since my first tumble into Underland only intensified after I left it for the second time. I would have thought it was just my imagination if it weren't for the fact that I actually saw my watchers. Mirrors were particularly prone to showing a flash of Underland: a flicker of red and gold here, a glimpse of Jack and his black-flecked eyes there. At first it was mostly Jack, his thin, arrogant face and perfectly pressed suits appearing and vanishing in windows and mirrors everywhere I went. I made faces at him whenever he appeared in the windows at school—which made him roll his eyes and sniff—and even a walk down the street was enough to display running scenes of Underland in the passing shop windows. I didn't recognise all of it by sight, but there was that kind of personal, friendly warmth to it that made me certain the sun there was alive, and that it could only be Underland. I caught a glimpse of Hatter and Hare quite often, but they were always so hard to see in the mirrors and windows. The light fractured around them, splitting the

23

glass into reflective shards, and the only reason I knew Hatter's face was because of his purple eyes.

I got a nasty shock once or twice, though. One night I woke at midnight to see a pale, pale face in the dressing mirror that was not my own, its crimson lips plump at the top and sharp at the bottom, almost as if its mouth were a heart. The Queen's eyes—for it was certainly she—were searching the mirror, falling inevitably into a line with my own. I closed my eyes with a gasp, fearful of meeting her gaze, and when I dared to open them again, she was gone. Her face had burned itself in the back of my eyes, however, and for many hours that night I lay awake with her strong, cruel face etched in the place where sleep should have been. Perhaps the most unsettling thing was that she looked so much like Jack. I should have expected it, but somehow I hadn't. There was a cruelness to Jack's face as well, and they both had that edge of madness to their eyes—though that, I was beginning to think, was simply an *Underland* thing rather than a familial thing—and the same pale gold hair.

I didn't last long in the foster home where I first saw the Queen. Maybe it was the sight of her, knowing she could find me so easily; that she could *see* me. Maybe it was my silent, prickly nature that made foster parents dislike me. Whatever it was, it saw me out of two foster homes in quick succession, and when I caught sight of the Queen in the next a few months later, I knew I wouldn't be long there. I began hanging clothes over the mirrors and twitching the curtains shut as soon as I went into my bedroom. It meant that I saw less of Jack, but that wasn't really a bad thing.

Hare and Hatter, on the other hand, I began to see a great deal more of. Though it was hard to see them in mirrors and windows, I saw them easily in anything curved and reflective; and most clearly in water. Before long, it was second nature for my eyes to linger on the puddles that I passed—though I was careful not to jump in them—and I spent most of my spare time reading beside whatever pond or creek that happened to be near my current foster home. Through the ripples I learned that though Hatter and Hare mostly remained by their tea table, they did a remarkable amount of work. Exactly what that work was I was never quite sure: visitors seemed to pop up at their table quite regularly. Much to my amusement, their method of 'popping up' was most often similar to mine. That big teapot saw a ridiculous amount of use, considering the pond close by. But sometimes the Hatter did something quick and sneaky with his hat that made things very difficult to see, even in the ripples. I watched and wondered: it seemed to me that whenever Hatter gazed at his hat with his mad purple eyes and made ripples, the Underland I saw in the ripples changed ever so slightly. I remembered Hatter saying that how Underland appeared depended upon the person doing the seeing, and on how they saw; and I wondered if Hatter was Seeing Things in a Different Way. And maybe changing things, little by little, just by Seeing them differently. I was too young to find the idea ridiculous, and I'd seen too much both in and *of* Underland to find it ridiculous by observation. I wanted to test it.

The next day after school, I wandered down to the creek behind the high school. I didn't want the twin boys I was sharing a foster home with to stumble over me, and since all of the high schoolers smoked beneath the overpass during periods, *they* wouldn't see me either. The creek ran shallow in a few sheltered spots where I could water-gaze without being disturbed. I found one of the quieter ones beneath the swaying fronds of a weeping willow, where the water eddied gently in a curved cut-out of the bank, and crawled in beneath the fronds. I had already been seeing flashes of Underland as I followed the stream, but when I settled on my stomach to gaze into the water properly, Hatter and Hare appeared immediately, sharp and clear. They weren't at their tea table; they were in a foresty part of Underland, dark and green and foreboding. Hatter and Hare looked distinctly out of place in it. Hare, for some incomprehensible reason, seemed to be carrying a crutch, and I saw Hatter's top hat as he passed close by my line of sight. In the ripply bit at the top of it I saw another view of him and Hare—this one of them walking in the sunny glade close by their tea table. They looked just the same but for their surroundings. I wondered if that other picture was what the Queen saw when she looked at them, and if so, *how*? What were they up to? They were talking to each other, but I couldn't hear what they were saying. I never did hear through the ripples, and I wasn't sure if that was because it wasn't possible, or if I just hadn't learned the trick of it yet. As I watched them they slipped silently into a darkened cave, heavy with shadow and sinister with dark mossy bones. It didn't look like a safe place to be. My reflected view took me through with them into the bare interior of the cave, where cobwebs soon began to drape from the walls and curved ceiling. At least, I *thought* they were cobwebs, until Hatter and Hare passed close by a particularly heavy patch and I discovered that they were actually wool. It was everywhere, draped in the corners and nooks, dangling from the ceiling in massive loops and tangles, forming giant dust-bunnies around the floor of the cave. I gazed at it, fascinated, and wondered if a cave hung with wool was any less frightening than a cave hung about with cobwebs, if they both had bones out the front. I was inclined to think that it was. In Underland you just didn't know what sort of madness you would meet with, and the kind of madness that had woollen cobwebs juxtaposed with human and animal bones was perhaps even more terrifying than that which had cobwebs. At least you expected cobwebs when it came to caves and bones.

The woollen cobwebs grew in size and fluffiness the further Hatter and Hare went. Soon they didn't even look like cobwebs anymore: they looked exactly what they were, great mountains of unwound wool heaped up toward the sides of the cave. I saw Hatter looking at the piles, and he seemed satisfied with them; but Hare was nervous, twitching, and inclined to tap against the cave floor with his powerful back legs as if he was preparing to run. That left me to wonder exactly who lived in a cave, apparently ate humans and animals alike, and had a passion for wool. Hatter and Hare didn't seem to concern themselves with the question: what I could read of Hatter's lips (Hare's were impossible to guess at) was merely the usual back and forth I was used to with them. It meant nothing and something at the same time.

I was so intent on trying to read their lips that I didn't notice the small thread of wool that seemed to be moving until the piles of wool ended abruptly and the single, taut, moving thread was the only skerrick of wool still to be seen against the darkness of the cave. It stretched far back into the darkness, still moving at a good speed, and as Hatter and Hare followed it, I began to see a vast glow of white something in the further recesses of the cave. Was that—could it be?—a mountain of *knitted wool*? And in front of it, a small white sheep, knitting. He almost blended into the mountain of wool, so similar were their colours, and although he looked quite sleepy, his hands manipulated his knitting needles so quickly that they were a blur. Hare still looked nervous, and even Hatter seemed watchful now, his purple eyes for once intent and focused. I curled my fingers into fists, vainly trying to tell what was happening, but they were only talking, and I couldn't even guess at what they were saying because I was at their backs. The sheep, whose face I *could* see, was impossible to read. His mouth wasn't formed for talking, and though the nonsense of Underland meant that he could and *did* talk, it didn't make it any easier to read his lips.

The first idea I had of something wrong was the sheep's knitting needles. They had been a blur, but now they stuttered and slowed. I saw Hare's big feet tap the rocky cave bottom twice, an unconscious twitch. His one good paw wrapped tightly around his crutch as though he was preparing to hit something with it. Hatter, very slowly, took off his hat. I found myself gripping handfuls of riverside grass, my fingers dirt-and-grass-stained, as the sheep's knitting needles slowed still more. I still couldn't tell what he was saying, but Hatter and Hare's body language said that when his knitting needles stopped completely, something very dreadful was going to happen.

Then his needles did stop. The little sheep slipped from his seat and stood upright, his knitting dropping to the ground. When the knitting hit the floor Hatter and Hare were already running, Hare bounding ahead on his powerful back legs and his crutch waving madly, and Hatter legging it with his top hat gripped in one hand. And then, from the mountain of knitting behind the sheep, something big and dreadful began to stir. Something that uncoiled to display claws and fangs of the sharpest...*wool*?

This huge, fanged, clawed beast arising from the knitting *was* the knitting. Only it didn't look soft and cuddly and stuffed. Its edges and curves were all deadly sharp, and there was a wicked gleam in its mad, knitted eyes. It wasn't like anything I had ever seen before. It wasn't dragon, or basilisk, or wyvern, though it looked a little like each.

My point of view was suddenly twitched around. Now I saw from the front as Hatter and Hare desperately pelted for the front of the cave, behind them a monstrosity in coloured wool leaping free of the white wool around it. Hatter's mouth said something like: "Jabberwock!" and in his eyes I saw deep, desperate fear. He didn't think they were going to make it.

"Run," I said, in a small, panting voice. They weren't moving anywhere near fast enough. The Jabberwock had fully uncoiled, and over their bobbing shoulders I saw it pounce forward, a terror of gaping mouth and arm-long teeth. "*Run!*" I screamed again. "Hatter, run!"

A painful show of light flooded the ripples as Hatter and Hare burst from the cave, the Jabberwock breathing hot over their shoulders. It threw the forest outside into high relief, and for a moment I saw the forest fold over the ripples, a piece of it disappearing in the fold.

It depends, Hatter had said; it depends on how it's Seen.

I reached out a shaking, grass-tattooed hand and pinched the forest between my fingers, making the rest of the forest disappear, just for a moment. Underland fractured, or drew together, or perhaps it really did fold. Hatter and Hare stumbled from the forest and into green hills—I released my pinch of Underland—the Jabberwock soundlessly howled its enraged disappointment to the forest canopy—and they were somehow safe. I sat up, my pulse thundering in my ears and my hand clasped to my chest, still dripping wet. Hatter and Hare, so far away yet so easily reached, looked as though they had gone mad —or maybe just madder. Hare was bounding in powerful, erratic circles, his legs kicking in mid-air and his crutch waggling at the sun, and Hatter seemed to be beating his top hat with one fist. I giggled as I watched them, and found that I was also crying. I had actually thought they were going to die. I had saved them—*had* I saved them? Was that me? Had I really reached into Underland and altered it? I looked from my hands to the water and back again, then at the water once more. Hatter had stopped beating his hat and was poking it with his fore-finger instead. He dipped his finger curiously in the ripply bit at the top and withdrew it slowly. Then he looked right at me, his purple eyes wide and wild and almost pupil-less. Ashamed of my tears, I scrambled to my feet and away through the weeping willow; but before Hatter quite vanished behind the sweeping greenery, I saw him smile.

5

___

I was an avid puddle-gazer from my ninth to my twelfth birthdays. No cards of invitation appeared on my pillow and I didn't accidentally fall into Underland either, so there seemed to be nothing for it but to watch from a distance. Then, at last, a few months after my twelfth birthday, I woke with a start to find that a playing card was on my pillow again. It kicked into gear a plan that must have been growing in my back brain for weeks. I snatched at the card, my thoughts spinning, and was out of the house less than fifteen minutes later. On my back was my school bag, stuffed with the food I'd hoarded over the last few weeks and heavy with as many clothes as I could manage. I'd stolen a carrot from the kitchen for Hare—a big fat one that seemed like it might make even him less loud and angry—and a patchwork cap I found in the dress-up bin at school for Hatter. Perhaps if I was clever about it, they would let me stay for a while.

But I didn't find them when I leapt into Underland. Instead, my puddle brought me out into a cool, dark woods. There was a chill to the air around my ankles, and dark green grass stretched

30

out in a velvety expanse beneath my shoes. Up ahead was a sharp demarcation of lighter green which I thought at first was a sunbeam finding its way through the trees, but turned out to be a straight line of lighter green grass. There was no graceful or patchy seguing between the two, it was a sharp, straight line; dark one side, light the other. Curious. I frowned at it, wondering if this was a sort of fake turf like the oval at school. Only why would there be fake grass in a wood?

"It's Underland," I said to myself, because I couldn't keep staring at it. I wanted to find Hatter and Hare. "Maybe the trees aren't real, either." I hefted my backpack a little higher on my back and walked toward the line of lighter green grass.

I had taken just one step over that line when a voice boomed: "Forfeit! Your life is forfeit! I claim this square!"

I clutched at the straps of my backpack, my heart racing, and saw a flash of red in the shadows. A furious thundering of hooves beat in my ears, and then my fear that the Queen had somehow found me again was put to flight by the very much more present danger of the red knight who was galloping straight at me. His horse was blood-red, too, its neck arched and proud, and there was a very sharp red lance pointed at my chest.

I froze for the barest instant, then threw myself sideways as the horse barrelled past, tearing up chunks of turf. The grass was soft and springy, and I rolled easily to my feet again despite my backpack. Unfortunately, in the time between rolling and rising, the red knight had pulled up, turned, and was setting his lance at me again.

"Ho! Challenger to the square!" called another voice behind me.

I gave a squeak, instinctively ducking, and a second horse and knight galloped past me, intent upon the red knight. This horse and knight were white, and when the red knight saw them, he spurred his own horse into a furious gallop again. My first feeling was one of relief. Maybe I could sneak away while they were fighting each other. The second was one of sudden terror: both knights had somehow utterly missed each other with their lances, and the red knight was still bearing down on me. I yelled and tried to leap sidewise again, but I was too slow. The red knight's lance slid between my shoulder and the strap of my backpack, burning me with its speed, and hove me off my feet.

For the briefest of moments, I flew. Then my weight dragged the point of the lance into the grass, and a red, shouting, clanking heap of metal sailed over my head and into a tree. There was the clashing of metal and wood, then a brief silence, during which I discovered that I was pinned to the grass by my backpack strap.

"Bravo!" shouted the white knight. "Oh, well played, madam! A rout indeed!"

"*Help!*" I said in annoyance.

The white knight at once dismounted. "A thousand pardons, madam! At once, and immediately!"

At once and immediately was not exactly how it happened. The white knight turned out to be incapable of helping me until he had removed his helmet and his gauntlets, which took far longer than it should have taken. Then he stopped to apologise for the necessity of touching me to remove the lance—'rude weaponry', he called it.

"*That's* all right," I said, eyeing his enormous white whiskers in fascination. "Just take it out, please. Why do you keep calling me madam?"

The white knight looked at me uncertainly. "Should I, perchance, address you as *sir*?"

"What? No! I'm a kid. I'm not even a miss yet. I'm Mabel."

"A great pleasure to meet you, Mistress Mabel," said the

white knight, at last plucking the lance from the earth beneath me. "I am Sir Blanc, wandering knight."

I took the hand he held out to me and rose to my feet a little shakily. "Thank you, Sir Blanc. You showed up just in time."

"Alas!" sighed Sir Blanc. "My interference has brought no glory! I have failed to bring about the downfall of my enemy."

"Well, neither did I," I said, throwing a look up at the red knight. "He went up, not down. And he did it to himself, anyway. Why did he attack me?"

"You approached his square," said Sir Blanc. "It was ever thus in the Chessboard Woods. He was honour bound to challenge you; as was I to challenge him. And yet, I failed!" He sank down on a fallen tree, a crumpled little tin can of sad eyes and drooping whiskers. "It's all of a piece," he continued, as if I wasn't there. "A failed knight, a failed inventor, always to be thwarted in my search."

He looked so woebegone that I was prompted to ask him: "What are you searching for?"

"My wits," he said sadly. "They wandered away and now I can't find them."

I said: "Oh," because there didn't seem to be anything else to say. In an effort to be helpful, I added: "Do you remember where you last had them?"

"I was envisioning my latest invention," said Sir Blanc meditatively. "Oh, very clever, it was! I've no idea what it's for *now*, but back when I had my wits about me I was a very clever fellow!"

"Your wits," I prompted, hugging my backpack.

"Indeed, indeed. I let my thoughts wander for a moment— pondering something devastatingly intelligent, methinks—and when I looked around my wits had wandered away."

"Just walked off, did they?" I wasn't quite sure that Sir Blanc wasn't making fun of me.

"The Queen had been waiting for just such an occasion,"

said Sir Blanc, his pleasant face darkening. "She swooped on them and took them away, and I've not seen them since."

I thought about this for far too long, until it occurred to me to ask: "Hang on, if the Queen has them, why are you looking for them *here*?"

"I know not," said Sir Blanc, even more sadly. "Forsooth, I've lost my wits! Alas the day! Once such a bright light in the rebellion!"

My eyes flew to his face. "What rebellion? The Queen came to the tea-party one day and—oh! Hatter and Hare! What rebellion, Sir Blanc?"

"It is gone with my wits," said Sir Blanc simply. "Until I regain my wits, I wander the Chessboard Woods and serenade the trees with my sad ditties."

"If the Queen has your wits, you won't find them by wandering the woods," I reminded him; but Sir Blanc wasn't listening. He was warbling something mournful to the greenery around us, his moustaches drooping disconsolately. "Where are Hatter and Hare?" I asked, by way of trying to stop the wavering noise. "Can you take me to them?"

"I fear not, Mistress Mabel. My wits, having fled, have taken with them all useful knowledge of my former associates and occupations."

"Maybe that's why the Queen took them," I said slowly. "When did your wits first go missing?"

"Five years ago," he said. "Five long, weary years!"

A fizz of excitement went through me. "That's when I came to Underland last! And the Queen was threatening Hatter and Hare. Maybe that's how she knew about them. Sir Blanc, if I help you get your wits back, will you take me to Hatter and Hare?"

"It would be my pleasure, madam."

"All right, then!" I said, pleased with myself. "Do you know how to get to the Queen's Castle?"

"Every man knows the path to the Castle of Hearts. That he may escape again from thence is another matter."

"Well, *we* will," I said stoutly. I couldn't see the red points of the Heart Castle from here in the woods, but the pall of it was still palpably felt. I had no intention of being trapped in it.

6

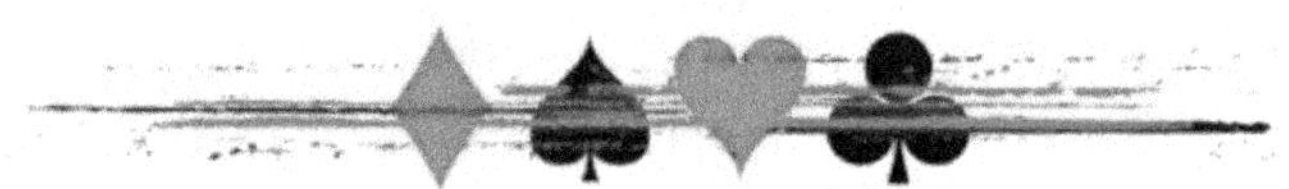

It took us a day and a half to get to the Heart Castle. We probably would have been faster walking, but Sir Blanc insisted on us riding his horse, which was so old and mournful that it seemed to take one step backwards for every two it took forwards, in a sort of a sad strathspey. I tried not to be irritated, because neither of them could really help it. Really, I could have made it to the Castle myself: it was immediately noticeable on the horizon when we got out of the Chessboard Woods. Unfortunately, Sir Blanc was too honourable to let me go by myself; *particularly* since I was helping him. I tried not to be irritated at that, too, but it was a bit harder: Sir Blanc may have been brave and kind, but he had no idea of how to be inconspicuous. It was partly his armour, which clanked and rattled more loudly than I'd thought possible; but he also had a habit of talking at the top of his lungs—or worse, when the dismals fell on him, softly wailing sad songs.

When we got to the Castle of Hearts, however, it became obvious that it would take a lot more than being inconspicuous to get in. Sir Blanc and I made it into the servants' courtyard without anyone batting an eyelid, but once there it was clear that the only thing getting past the guards and into the Castle itself were recognised servants and a series of heavily weighed and loudly creaking metal carts. Each of them was guarded by a red knight who stood to attention on a metal footboard at the back of the carts, and each of them was pulled by a stocky little mechanical horse. I wondered at the mechanical horses until it occurred to me that real horses needed drivers, and there was no room on the carts for a driver. They seemed to be very precise in their movements, and no less precise in their timing: an outgoing cart met an incoming cart on the hour, every hour. I counted the minutes on my watch, which interested Sir Blanc greatly, looking around at the courtyard while we waited. It had been made into a storage ground for various stockpiles of supplies, from barrels of wine to crates of apples, and a lunch spot for a lot of very small, very grimy children. Sir Blanc and I lingered close to the apples and tried to think of a way past the guards. At least, I tried to think of a way past the guards while Sir Blanc became enthralled by my watch, which I had given him to distract him from his very loud determination to challenge the red knights to combat. When he was enthralled enough to have forgotten about the other knights, I stole one of the apples from the crates and sidled up to one of the kids.

Munching on my apple, I jerked my chin at the latest cart and said: "What's that?"

"An ice cart."

"Why's it getting into the castle? They're not letting anyone else in."

"It's for them ice vents in the castle: they keep the halls cool in the summer. The ice goes in the ice chamber and a bunch of vents splits off from there and runs through the castle so it all stays cool."

"Oh, that's clever," I said, thinking of the air conditioning systems back in Australia. They were probably better at keeping places cool, but it wasn't very likely that you could sneak in through the air conditioning. I was very much hoping that it *would* be possible to sneak through the ice vents. The only question was to get into the ice chamber itself. I was quite certain that wandering into the ice chamber with a knight would be even harder than sneaking into the castle with one. Unless...unless I didn't try to sneak in with a *white* knight. Unless I tried to sneak in with a *red* knight.

Sir Blanc, for all his clanking and vagueness, proved to be very handy when it came to waylaying one of the carts and its attendant knight. Maybe the loss of his wits made him more prone to violence. We attacked it a street before it turned into the courtyard, and while Sir Blanc did most of the hard work, I was proud of the fact that it was I who unseated the red knight from his position with my school tie. Once he was on the cobbles in a stunned heap, it was Sir Blanc who removed his helmet and hit him once, very effectively, in the head. He also proved to be very good with knots, and had the red knight trussed and out of sight in an alley before the cart had a chance to turn into the courtyard.

While Sir Blanc settled himself on the moving cart, wrapped in the red knight's cloak and wearing his helmet, I scrambled into the back, where I was simultaneously almost crushed and almost frozen by the massive block of ice it contained. From there it was simply a matter of listening anxiously to Sir Blanc's short interaction with the castle guards, and excitedly to the sound of our progress echoing against the passage walls as we drove into the bowels of the castle.

We drove for a lot longer than I expected, making a curved descent that seemed to be never-ending and increasingly claustrophobic until, all at once, the noise of the cart again echoed loudly. Shortly after, the mechanical horse stopped, though the sound of its clopping remained while Sir Blanc descended from his perch and lifted me out of the cart.

"We're in!" I said. I couldn't quite believe it myself. I looked around us while the mechanical horse waited patiently for its load to be uncrated. The ice chamber was enormous, cold reflecting off the domed metallic surface. To my joy, the vents that dimpled it at regular intervals were large enough not only to fit my skinny body, but Sir Blanc's much larger one. There were even ladders leading to the higher vents. Well, air vents must have to be cleaned and repaired occasionally, I supposed. The chill that surrounded us from the massive blocks of ice already unloaded was something fierce.

"Very well," said Sir Blanc. "Where shall we begin, madam? I am entirely at your disposal."

"The royal chambers, I suppose," I said. "Where are they?"

"We must traverse two levels of underlings and utility chambers before we attain to the galleries and royal chambers."

"All right," I said, throwing another look around. "The higher vents, then."

It hadn't really occurred to me how horribly noisy Sir Blanc would be when confined to a metallic vent. If he was noisy out in the open air, he was actually *shattering* in the metal vent system. It wasn't easy getting him in the vent, either. And when I tried to warn him about the amount of noise, he looked reproachfully at me and said: "A knight and a nobleman does not creep into a fortress like a sneak-thief, Mistress Mabel. My honour much misgives me."

"Your honour is helping a damsel in distress," I told him crossly, and kept crawling. It was *half* true. "And my name is Mabel. Not mistress or madam."

"Certainly, my dear child," responded Sir Blanc, once more conveniently oblivious. Redirecting his thoughts wasn't hard, but it was a little wearisome having to do it so often. "Shall we arrive soon, do you think?"

"Don't know," I panted. "Hold on, Sir Blanc: boost me up to this grating. I think I can see a grand hall."

It *was* a grand hall, like something out of a fairy tale book. Red knights lined a hall of marbled white and scarlet, and a grating opposite me in my line of sight told me that if we continued straight ahead, we would be going in the wrong direction. As we travelled toward the castle through a giant chessboard of different shades of green, Sir Blanc had told me that the Queen kept all her exotic curios in a small room at the centre of the castle, close to the royal chambers. He had been beamingly surprised when I suggested that it was possible she kept his wits there, too.

"Which way to the Queen's curio room from the grand hall?" I hissed down at him.

"Onward and upward!" said Sir Blanc, by far too loud. I thought one of the red knights might have moved at the noise, but I didn't stay to be sure. Instead, Sir Blanc and I continued onward and upward, taking each passage that led us higher until we came to an exceedingly tiny grate on the inward-facing side of the passage. I'd noticed that the grates usually had a counterpart on the opposite side of whichever room we found ourselves, but this grate had none. It was also by far the smallest grate we had yet seen. I couldn't see through it at all until I realised that it was double-grated: there was another grate further in, at least an arms-length away. When I pried out the grating on my side, I could see the marble bricks that formed the rectangular hole; and through that, a small piece of a plush, velvety sort of room that seemed to be almost entirely red.

"I think we found it!" I said, in an excited whisper. What I could see of the room was lined with glass-covered shelves, behind which were myriad tiny knick-knacks and oddities. In one corner I could see the contours of curving red wood that I could imagine were heart-shaped doors.

"What a shame we can't fit through this grate! It must be the right one: *she* wouldn't leave anything up to chance. What do you think we should do?"

Sir Blanc carefully let me down, and stared at the hole for a long, thoughtful moment.

"We must find a troupe of tiny people!" he said at last, his eyes bright. "We shall enlist their good services by representing to them the iniquity of the Heart Queen's reign of terror."

He looked so pleased with himself that I didn't like to bring him down to earth. Well, for all I knew, Underland *might* be home to a troupe of tiny people. They weren't *here*, though, and I didn't much like our chances of getting back into the Heart Castle once we were safely out again.

"That's a good plan," I said, smiling at him. "But supposing we can't find a troupe of tiny people in time? Maybe we can find another grating that's close enough to sneak into the room without anyone seeing us."

Sir Blanc gave me a sad, sweet smile. "It was a terrible plan, wasn't it? My regrets, dear child: I am of no use to you."

"That's not true! I wouldn't have been able to get in here without you! Who knocked out the guard, and tied him up? Who boosted me up into all these vents?"

Sir Blanc, after thinking about it, said in a pleased sort of a way: "'Twas myself, forsooth!"

"That's right," I said, descending from rhetoric to particulars to avoid confusing him: "And you stopped the red knight from killing me, too. Look, if we crawl up the right-hand vent, we can probably skirt around the side of it and sneak into the halls."

"A knight does not sneak," said Sir Blanc.

"Well, I'll sneak. You just try not to clank."

Music filtered into the vents the further we crawled. We were getting close, I knew.

"What do you see, child?" hissed Sir Blanc. He was still too loud, but at least he wasn't clanking so much now. We were quickly approaching another grating, just as I thought we would. When I finally wriggled up to it, I found that it looked out on a small antechamber. It was a cool room for tray upon tray of tiny finger food and beautifully coloured bottles of wine. Unfortunately, even such a tiny room wasn't unoccupied. Leaning against the doorway was a tall, thin figure with razor-sharp creases in his trousers and shiny red shoes with pointy toes. He was holding a champagne glass with something red and bubbly in it, but he wasn't drinking: it seemed to be more of an elegant accessory. I'd seen him so often in windows and reflections that I recognised him straight away, even from behind.

I whispered to Sir Blanc: "Hang on. I might be able to get us some help."

We were certainly in the right place: the wide doorway Jack was leaning into had heart-shaped mouldings that opened out at about waist height, and beyond that I could see the curve of red heart-shaped doors. Much to my joy, there were no card sharks in sight. Unfortunately, the lack of card sharks was probably due to the fact that the room beyond the antechamber was full of laughing, drinking guests. No one could get into that room without being seen by at least a dozen people. I couldn't shout, either, or the guests would hear me. Whispering, on the other hand, wouldn't draw Jack's attention over the babble of conversation and the wail of the violin.

I settled for a piercing hiss. "Oi! Jack!"

One golden brow arched as Jack's head turned. His black-flecked eyes searched the space behind him, flickering over red and white marble until they came to rest on the decorative grating that I crouched behind. Perhaps he was going to ignore me—or perhaps he hadn't really figured out where the noise was coming from—because he turned back to the music room, his eyes running lazily over the room. At length, however, he turned around again, his eyes lingering on the other room, and sauntered casually toward me. He gave the clasp a quick, sharp kick with the heel of his shiny red shoes, his eyes never leaving the other room and his back never losing its arch.

In fact, the only acknowledgement he gave of my presence as I crawled out of the ice vent was to say: "*Don't* get mud on my shoes, Mab!"

"They're too shiny anyway," I said disapprovingly.

"What are you doing, exactly?"

"I need your help."

"Well, hello, how are you, and good to see you too!"

That threw me enough off balance to silence me for a moment. Then I said cautiously: "Hello. How are you?"

"More than slightly bored," said Jack, his eyes still roving the room. "Thank you for asking. Mother dearest has been called away briefly, so I'm hosting the most boring party Underland has ever seen. No, stay down there: if you get up they'll be able to see your head above the mouldings."

I settled my backside down in the shaft again and hugged my knees.

"I see you're still grubbing about under tables and in—what *is* that, exactly?"

"These are the ice vents," I said, surprised. "It's how this place stays so cool. Didn't you know?"

"Obviously not," said Jack, a little stiffly. "Are you still keeping bad company?"

"I don't keep bad company," I told him, with equal stiffness. Something sharp prodded my backside, prompting me to squeak and tumble out of the vent, and Sir Blanc exited behind me, pointy helmet foremost.

Jack, his eyes very narrow, only said: "So I see."

"Salutations, Emissary of the Red Heart!" said Sir Blanc, far too loudly. Jack winced, and my own eyes flew to the main room.

"Sir Blanc, *shhhh!*"

"Evil must never be confronted in silence, dear child," Sir Blanc said, in gentle reproof.

Jack became very still, radiating offense from every sharp edge. "What are you doing here, Mab?"

"We're stealing back Sir Blanc's wits," I told him, wondering if I should apologise. "The Queen took them, and he needs them back for, for—well, he needs them back."

"I see. And what do you want with me?"

"See that door?" I pointed to where the heart-shaped door of the Queen's curio room could be seen over the curve of the moulding. "We need you to make a distraction so that we can get in there."

"In these clothes?" Jack touched a slender hand to the blood-red ruby in his perfectly arranged cravat, his pale brows arched in polite disbelief. "Certainly not! Make your own distraction. As a matter of fact, if you wander into that crowd in those filthy rags, you'll make as big of a distraction as you could hope for."

"How about I step on your fancy red shoes?" I suggested. "Will that cause a distraction?"

Jack gave me a cold look, but Sir Blanc shuffled forward in a series of dull clanks and patted me kindly on the head.

"Rail not, sweet child. We do not require this varlet's services."

"Oh, it's varlet now, is it?" said Jack, eyeing Sir Blanc in dislike. "I can see you've been endearing yourself, Mab. He seems to think you're some sort of a dog. Ow! *Mab!*"

"Keep talking," I said grimly. "See what happens!"

Jack threw a swift look around, and then crouched beside me. "One day, Mab–!"

I stared at him stonily. "One day *what*?"

"Well, for starters, one day we're going to be married, and I won't have you grubbing about in ice-vents dressed like an undermaid."

"We're not going to be married!"

Jack sighed. "I know I explained it to you, Mab. I was nine, you were a toddler...blood, bonding ceremony, Mother Dearest?"

"*That?* That means we're going to be married?"

"Exactly. Thankfully, not for some years yet."

I stared at him until I was certain he wasn't laughing at me, then said firmly: "No."

Much to my surprise, Jack abandoned the subject without further argument. "I'll make a distraction," he said, rising. "But if that tinpot makes so much as one *clank* while I'm distracting them, and it gets back to Mother Dearest that I've been colluding with idiots and inebriates–"

"Hey!"

"That, varlet, is grounds for a meeting!"

Jack threw him a mocking look and sauntered back into the other room. I thought for a sharp, fearful moment that he was going to give us away for spite, but then I heard his voice slip into a soft, caramel purr. "It seems a shame to have such a renowned musician here and not take the opportunity of utilising his services," he said. Or perhaps he sang it: there was a depth and roundness to his voice that made it carry across the whole room. "Hearts and Diamonds, your entertainer: Cat Cheshire!"

His voice must have been well-known. I heard gasps of delight and clapping hands, then the whole of the party rustled and swayed their way to the left side of the room, clustering around the piano, Jack, and Cat Cheshire.

Sir Blanc started to climb to his feet, but I tugged at his left gauntlet.

"Not until he starts singing!" I whispered. Jack was right: Sir Blanc was entirely too noisy. Hopefully Cat Cheshire was a robust performer, or we were both going to be caught. Fortunately, the piano began to play a sly, off-beat blues number with a backing of trumpets, quite loud enough to hide the noise of Sir Blanc's sneaking, and I stepped lightly into the other room with the white knight right behind me.

Through the glittering, shifting crowd I could see Jack. He was standing beside the black-skinned, blue-sequined man who was playing the piano, his eyes flickering around the room. I supposed he was there to make sure everyone was looking at Cat Cheshire, though why anyone would be looking away from him was the first thought that sprang to my mind. Cat Cheshire, in addition to his blue-sequined suit, had a blue-sequined hat and a pair of dark glasses. He also had a trick of twitching to the music that was eye-catching. I hoped it meant that he wouldn't see Sir Blanc and me, and wished that he would start singing. Sir Blanc had a bad habit of clanging *between* blasts of the trumpets rather than while they were happening. But when the singing started, it was Jack's voice that I heard: deep, smooth, and effortlessly breathtaking. More than that, it was mesmerising. I didn't realise that I had stopped to stare, my mouth open, until Jack's eyes caught mine and he smirked at me. Then I blinked a little, shut my mouth, and pressed onward to the heart door. It seemed wrong that such a beautiful voice belonged to such an annoying boy.

I didn't quite let out my breath until the red heart door closed silently behind us. The music softened, much to my secret disappointment, but I could still faintly hear the thrum of Jack's voice and the purl of the trumpets. Around us was a red and white room with soft edges: plush carpet, plump furniture, and curved wooden shelving. I had the feeling that I could easily sink into it all if I wasn't careful. Even Sir Blanc's clanking wasn't as bad in here.

"All right, Sir Blanc," I said to him. "Where are your wits?"

Sir Blanc looked around vaguely. "Assuredly, they're in the room. I feel them. I am certain I shall know them if once I have them in my hand."

I had to bite the inside of my cheek before I could say with any patience at all: "Do you want to go through all the shelves and pick up everything?"

"An exceedingly good proposal!" cried Sir Blanc.

"We'll start with the ones in glass cases," I told him, sighing. "Those will be the most valuable ones. And we'll only pick up the ones that are made up of more than one piece."

A smile overspread Sir Blanc's usually doleful face. "Forsooth! A clever ruse indeed; my wits numbering more than one!"

"That's what I'm hoping," I said.

There were so many glass-fronted shelves. We began by the heart doors, grubbing up the glass-fronted cabinets there with my fingerprints while I plucked every likely curio from the shelves and plopped them into Sir Blanc's waiting hands. He giggled at some, cooed at others, and said "Forsooth!" every so often, but he didn't seem to recognise any of the items. When we got to the wall opposite the doors there was a small gap between curio cases that featured a tiny, round table with a frosted-glass cover over it and a small, decorative grating peeking through its spindly legs. It was the opening we'd seen from the inside of the ice-vents: a small, brick-sized grating that hid a small, brick-sized opening back into the vent system. Cool air flowed from it, promising freedom that was impossible to get to. The wall was simply too thick.

"Pity we can't shrink ourselves," I said regretfully, running my fingers over the glassy knob on top of the glass cover. At least we had Jack on the outside to get us back out, but I wasn't looking forward to sneaking past that crowd again. Jack had stopped singing, too, which was a pity. It wasn't something I'd ever tell him, but his voice was one of the most beautiful things I'd ever heard. You didn't expect to hear a smooth bass from such a narrow, sharp-faced boy. More to the point, while he wasn't singing, the crowd wasn't distracted.

"Eh?" said Sir Blanc. He was hovering over a crystal carafe of something that was sitting invitingly on a display table in the middle of the room. It even had a couple of glasses by it. More worryingly, it had a tag on it that read: *Drink Me.*

"Never mind," I said, lifting the frosted-glass cover I'd found.

I knew right away that I'd found Sir Blanc's wits. There were about six of them, and they looked like little beans. Well, little beans with...little shoes. And little feet in them, with little legs. I heard one of them squeak, and then they were off, tearing across the table and leaping to the floor. They were so quick that I could only catch one of them, its legs windmilling madly as it tried to catch up with the others.

"Hah!" said Sir Blanc in some satisfaction. "They were ever quick wits! Post-haste, child! Seize them!"

I thrust the frosted-glass cover at him, upside down and with the single captured wit in it, and chased after the other five. They were quick and nimble, and they had the advantage of being able to run under the furniture that I had to run around, but I was quick and nimble too. I captured another two of them when they made the mistake of crossing a rug that was even deeper than the carpet, and I was closing in on a third that was running for the door when someone thumped on the wooden panels. Sir Blanc and I both froze: it wasn't a loud thump, but it was very distinct. It sounded as though someone had leaned against the lintel and accidentally bumped their elbow against the door. I motioned at Sir Blanc to be very quiet, but he was too busy playing with the three captured wits to notice, so I pounced on the one I had cornered and added it to his bowl before I crept back to the door. When I cracked it open just a little the first thing I saw was a sleek red jacket. I went limp in relief. It was only Jack.

"What do you want?" I hissed.

Jack barely glanced over his shoulder, which was blocking the other room from me as much as it was blocking me from the other room. "Are you finished? Mother Dearest won't be long."

"I've got four of them, but the other two are hiding behind one of the cabinets and won't come out."

"Well, hurry it up," said Jack, peeling himself away from the door and straightening his cuffs. "She won't be away forever."

I'd rounded up the last two wits with enough time to be impatient by the time I heard a soft knock on the door again. I'd even managed to stuff them all into my pockets, where they wriggled and squeaked and generally made me feel uncomfortable. I could have put them in my backpack, but I was afraid they would escape. I cracked the door open only to see Jack's shoulders again, so I slipped my finger through the opening and poked him in the ribs.

"Oi! We're ready to go! Better start singing again."

He stiffened, but didn't jump. "My voice is tired," he said over his shoulder.

"What do you mean?" I demanded, in deep suspicion.

"I do wish you wouldn't run at things like a bull at a gate!" complained Jack. "Where's your subtlety, Mab? I'm *clearly* trying to extort something from you."

"Well, I wish you wouldn't talk like a dictionary," I said grumpily. "But I don't reckon that's going to change, so why should I? What do you want?"

"I need something from you, you need something from me. How about a trade?"

I gazed at his shoulders with an open mouth. "You waited until we were in here to bargain!"

"Of course I did," said Jack. "I'm not a fool. Are you ready to listen?"

"Listen to *what*?"

"My mother picked you out when I was a child–"

"Picked me out? You mean kidnapped!"

"–for the purpose of an engagement," continued Jack, as if I hadn't spoken. "That engagement is pretty widely known around Underland, and it's as widely known that we'll be married on my twenty-fifth birthday."

"*Engagement*," I said bitterly. I still had nightmares about that night. "She took my blood. People don't swap blood when they get engaged. They swap rings. Why did she mix our blood, anyway?"

Jack shrugged easily, his shoulder briefly revealing and then obscuring the room again. "Just an old tradition. Nothing important. But it does mean something to her. She's determined to see us married."

"You don't have to do what she tells you to do," I said. "You're almost grown up."

"The rules are the rules," said Jack. "I have to follow the rules. What I *do* with the rules, now: that's a different matter entirely. We've got a better chance if we join forces. You promise that you won't disappear, promise that you'll come back to marry me when it's time, and I'll make another distraction so you can get out before Mother Dearest comes back."

"You said we could run," I said. "I remember. That first time, when she mixed our blood, you said that we had a lot of time for running."

"I was wrong," said Jack, with something of a grimness in his voice. "There's no future in running. Literally. Mother Dearest's Mirror Hall was quite...*clear*...on that."

"What if I want to marry someone else?"

Black-flecked eyes came to bear on my face. "Who do you want to marry?"

"I don't know, I'm only twelve!"

"Well, then! Promise!"

"No," I said. "You're not very nice and if I break my promise later on that means *I'm* not very nice."

"I've never been very nice and I'm not likely to begin now," said Jack. "It's best if you give up on that. I am very good at staying alive, however, and that should count for something."

"I'm not going to promise," I said in dislike.

"Well, I'm not going to get you out," said Jack, shrugging elegantly. "You'll have to find your own way out."

"I *will* then!" I hissed, pulling the door sharply shut. I heard the slight thump and Jack's exclamation as he was pulled off balance, and smiled. Serve him right.

Sir Blanc, who was watching me with some anxiety, said, "Dear child, I am very much afraid that I've led you into a very sticky situation."

"Can we put your wits back in?"

"I regret to say that we cannot. It requires someone in possession of a competent hand with a needle: perhaps a dressmaker."

"What, *sew* them back in?"

"It is the only way," said Sir Blanc simply. "A method tried and true for shadows, wits, and reputations."

"What about a hatter? Could a hatter do it?"

"Forsooth, were it *The* Hatter, certainly."

"All right," I said, thinking very quickly. It wouldn't be long before the Queen joined the party, and Sir Blanc and I couldn't still be here when she arrived. "So we just have to get out of here first."

"Indeed," sighed Sir Blanc. He sat himself down desolately

on the Queen's coffee table, gazed soulfully around the room, and gave every sign of breaking into a sad song at any moment.

"I have an idea," I said quickly. I had found myself in front of the tiny ice-vent again. "But you'll have to be very quiet. It's trying to wriggle away, and I need to grab it while I can."

Sir Blanc looked mildly hopeful. That was good. The more cheerful he was, the less likely he was to burst into doleful ditties. And I really did have an idea—or at least, *part* of one— that was doing its best to wriggle away between the cracks of my mind. Wriggle? No, *ripple*. That was what my mind was catching on. I had watched the Hatter and his ripply hat somehow change things in Underland, and I had changed things myself. Somewhere at the back of my mind was the idea that if I could See Things Differently today, too, perhaps I could use the ripples to change things again.

"I need water," I said to Sir Blanc.

"I myself am a little parched," he said. "Unhappily, I see no water here."

"What about that?" I asked, pointing the crystal carafe of *Drink Me*.

Sir Blanc's brow creased. "I caution against indulging in that libation dear child. Dear me, no! It declares: 'drink me'. I have not all my wits about me, but that is a risk I am not willing to chance."

"I don't want to drink it," I said, pouring a measure of the clear liquid into a smooth, transparent glass. I thought I saw Jack's face briefly in it, but the swirl of liquid did away with it quickly. I carried it carefully over to the ice-vent and nestled it into the red carpet while I tore off the grating with my fingertips.

"I hesitate to point this out, my child, but I fear that you are marginally too large for such a mode of egress."

"I know," I said, and went back to my glass. If I lay on my side in the carpet and looked at the vent through the liquid, it looked much larger. Perhaps if I could See it differently, it would *be* different.

"Go through the vent, Sir Blanc," I told him, my eyes steadily on the enlarged vent. There was a series of clankings behind me as he stood again, then a tiny armoured Sir Blanc was climbing into the vent in front of me.

"Astounding!" he said, his moustaches quivering with excitement. "Who could have imagined!"

"I've seen Hatter do it," I said, pink and gruff with embarrassment. "It's nothing special. Keep going, Sir Blanc; I'm coming."

Everything went a bit wobbly when I got up. For a sick-making moment it was impossible to tell whether everything had gotten bigger or if Sir Blanc and I had simply gotten smaller. I seemed to walk past a giant glass of liquid to climb into the vent, and the carpet was huge and lumpy behind us; but when we dropped back into the main vent system from the smaller outlet it was no larger than it had been before. The wits, on the other hand, were still wriggling as vehemently as before, and their squeaks seemed to echo around the vent as loudly as Sir Blanc's clangings. This in turn made Sir Blanc shift uncomfortably, so I sent him on ahead to see if the mechanical horse was still waiting for us and explored the vents a little more thoroughly while I was at it. It had occurred to me that with Sir Blanc's wits still not available to him, I would have no one to take me to the Hatter and Hare. It was my fault, of course. I'd assumed that Sir Blanc's wits would be able to go right back in— though now I came to think of it, I did wonder *how*, exactly— and that he would be able to lead me to Hatter and Hare. Instead, he would need Hatter just to sew his wits back in, and neither of us had the slightest idea of where to find Hatter. Jack, on the other hand, almost certainly knew where Hatter and Hare's tea table was in relation to the Castle, so I spent some time shuffling about in the vents until I found his room. The grating I found would be a little more challenging to get out of: it looked down on the room from a rather high ceiling. It wasn't exactly a room, though—it was a whole *lot* of rooms. Jack had a whole suite to himself. It was bigger than most of the foster homes I'd stayed in. I had a certain amount of satisfaction in thinking that to exit I would have to bounce down on Jack's perfectly made bed. I gazed at it enviously from behind my grating, taking in the black and white marbled floors, the white rugs throughout, and the heavy blackness of the plain rectangular bed. There wasn't a flash of red to be seen in the entire suite.

A card man came in while I was still gawking and made me jump, but he was only there to run a bath, which seemed like a good thing. If Jack was having a bath run, it wouldn't be long before he showed up. I'd better return to Sir Blanc while I could. If I could be sure he was in a safe place, wits and all, it would be easy enough to wait here until the party was over and Jack returned to his suite. Accordingly, I made my way swiftly back through the ice-vents, making turn after carefully remembered turn until my feet were on the rungs of the ladder that led back down into the ice chamber. Sir Blanc greeted me happily, and as happily agreed to wait for me outside both castle and city streets. We had left his horse at a small way-station about half a day's journey from the gates. It wasn't much more than a roof and a bit of straw, but it had been comfortable enough to spend the night in, and both of us knew where to find it again. I repeated my instructions to Sir Blanc twice anyway, just to be sure, and tucked his recovered wits into the pocket at the front of his gambeson.

"Don't let them out!" I said. "Not even if they squeak."

"I shall not," said Sir Blanc solemnly. "How will you escape, child?"

"I have another way out," I told him, hoping as I said it that it was true. I helped him back onto the mechanical cart just before the horse began to move and hoped that no one would notice the dripping ice-water that showed its cargo was still on board.

I climbed more quickly this time, sure of my way. It wouldn't help to remember the way after today, of course: the Queen would make sure no one entered the castle by the ice vents again when she discovered the missing wits. But I found myself reinforcing the memories anyway, counting off the turns and the ladders as I went. Jack's bedroom suite caught up with me even more quickly than I expected, and soon I was looking down on his bed again, calculating the jump in my mind. The card servant was gone, which was convenient: it meant that I could rattle the grate free without being overheard. I wanted to be ready when Jack came back. When the grate was out, I put it carefully beside me in the vent, rubbing my hands against each other to ward off the chill in the air. Then I waited.

It wasn't long before Jack sauntered into the room, his red suit coat hung over his arm. I leapt as soon as he carelessly shut the door behind him, landing lightly but bouncing a bit more than I expected to bounce. I *had* hoped to make him jump. Instead, Jack merely laid his coat over the back of a plush black chair, straightened his cuffs, and advanced into the bedroom.

"I thought you might come back," he said.

"You're no fun," I said sourly.

"What, because I didn't jump through the roof?" He saw me briefly wrinkle my nose in annoyance, and laughed. "I'll have to tell Mother to block those vents."

"Why didn't she block them already? If a kid and a witless knight can get in, who can't?"

"Because she understands Underland. She knows how people think. No—she *determines* how people think. She's very good at it, and she spends a lot of time in the Mirror Hall."

"She doesn't determine how I think!" I said in annoyance. I still saw the Mirror Hall quite often in my puddle-gazing. In fact, the more I saw of it, the more it seemed to me that it was somewhere the Queen shouldn't be allowed. Things were different there. Seen differently. Made differently. The Queen herself Saw and Made things that were contrariwise to what actually Was.

"I'm beginning to feel that the only way she *could* do that would be to tell you to think the exact opposite. Perhaps she is. She's incredibly off-putting that way. Shall I tell you stories of when I was a lad: how she tricked me into punishing myself?"

I didn't like the black look to his eyes, or the unpleasant tilt to his mouth. He was only eighteen. He shouldn't look like that.

I said: "If you knew I'd be here, why did you come back so early? I can still hear the party."

"It wasn't for the pleasure of your company, if that's what you mean. How did you get out of Mother's curio room? I'd have sworn there was no way out but the door."

"None of your business!" I said. I was beginning to feel that it was a mistake to come back, but I had to know how to get to Hatter and Hare.

"Well, that's rude," said Jack. "I suppose you want to know how to get to your other little friends? Or did you come back because you want to hear me sing again? I didn't peg you as a music-lover, Mab!"

"Call *that* music, do you?" I said scornfully, but Jack's odiously self-satisfied smile didn't even waver. "Sounded like a calf yelling for its mum."

"Has it ever occurred to you, Mab, that your method of obtaining help leaves a little something to be desired?"

After a brief, exasperated pause, I said: "Yes. But you're *so annoying* that I just can't help myself."

"That," said Jack, "Is the most egregious example of the pot calling the kettle black that I have ever heard. Do you or do you not want to find your friends?"

"I do."

"Very well: follow me. I've made preparations."

Maybe I shouldn't have followed him so trustingly, but I did. We didn't go far: just to the bathroom, where the drawn bath was waiting.

"Hey!" I said indignantly. "I might not be as squeaky clean as you, but I don't need a bath!"

"I could beg to differ, but I won't. Whether or not you need a bath is entirely beside the point."

I looked suspiciously at him. "What is the point, then?"

"I've got an idea," said Jack. "If I did it myself it would be against the rules, but it wouldn't be against the rules for you. And I have another idea that says you've probably already started practising by yourself."

"How did you know about the ripples?"

"Call it intuition," said Jack. "Only not in front of anything that doesn't ripple. Mother can only use the flat reflective ones, so it should be safe enough."

"You mean I can talk to Hatter and Hare through the bathwater? I've never *heard* them before. And I don't *try* to see them; it always just sort of happens."

"Which is why we're starting with the bathtub rather than the wash-basin," said Jack. "Much easier to work with. Oh, and also because of the vanity mirror over there."

"You've put a towel over it," I said, after a wild, frightened look at it.

"Yes, and that reminds me: stop making faces at me when I come to visit you."

"Visit? You mean *spy!*"

Jack shrugged. "A rose by any other name..."

"A rose by any other name still has as many thorns," I said. "How do I call up Hatter and Hare?"

"For a start, you don't *call them up*," said Jack, propping himself against the bathroom wall slightly behind and beside me. "It's not calling, it's seeing. They're there all the time, you just have to be able to see them. As for being able to hear them, so long as you're actively Seeing instead of passively seeing, there's no reason you shouldn't hear them, too."

"What do you mean, actively?"

"I mean trying as opposed to merely watching things as they stream," said Jack. "Indolent little thing, aren't you, Mab? See them. Make the ripples do what you want them to do."

"Hatter told me about Seeing," I said thoughtfully. "About Underland being a reflection of what we see—oh!"

"DORMY!" yelled a familiarly frenzied voice. And then there they were, in the ripples: Hatter and Hare in all their gloriously mad familiarity. Maybe Jack was right about me being lazy. It hadn't really taken much to see them.

I couldn't help the glad smile that spread across my face. "Hatter! Hare! I found you! It's me!"

Hatter's purple eyes were wild and a little bit watchful, but he didn't speak. It was left to Hare to add, at a bellow: "WHAT BIG EARS YOU HAVE, DORMY!"

I looked back at Jack in confusion, and found that he was looking exasperated. He mouthed at me: *They're being watched.* I mouthed back at him: *Can I be seen?*

Jack shook his head while Hatter and Hare waited. I would have liked to have asked him if I could be heard by anyone watching them, but since he was already taking pains not to be heard and Hatter and Hare were talking in riddles more than usual, the answer was pretty obvious.

Carefully, I said: "I've got a friend who'd like you to sew him a new, um, hat. He says you sew things very well. Only he can't leave home at the moment."

"Hatters do not make house calls," said Hatter. "You're thinking of a doctor."

"Well, if you think a doctor can sew better..." I let the sentence trail off, and saw Hare bristle.

"HATTER CAN SEW ANYTHING FROM REPUTATIONS TO WITS," he said loudly.

"No, you're thinking of owls," I said, hoping that they would understand. "They're the ones that make to-whits and to-whos."

"I can sew a hat for an owl," said Hatter, his eyes intent upon me and his pupils dilating. "Is it a very big owl? White? Black? Red? I'll need to bring the right thread, you know."

"White," I said, dizzy with relief. Hatter *had* understood. "And very big. He's staying at a little waystation outside the Heart Castle."

"Good place for an owl," Hatter said, and I felt warm with approval even though his tone was aloofly disinterested. "Lots of straw. Lots of mice."

"He's expecting you," I said.

I wanted to say so much more. I wanted to tell Hatter that I'd seen them face the Jabberwock—that I'd seen them escape— that I'd *helped* them escape. I wanted to tell them that I missed them. I wanted to pass right through the ripples, and I had the feeling that maybe I could do it if I went right now. I made a tiny, involuntary movement forward, my fingers dipping toward the water, and then Jack's hand was on my shoulder, fingers sharp and prohibitive. If he had been trying to keep out of sight, he'd just ruined it: Hatter and Hare must have seen him. They didn't blink, but they faded from sight almost immediately.

"Oh," I said sadly, feeling deflated. "They're gone!"

"They are," said Jack, his hand still gripping my shoulder. "And it's time that you were going, too, Mab."

He lunged for me so quickly that I was too surprised to defend myself. In short order I found myself bundled into an unwieldy ball of backpack, clothes, and limbs, held firmly in

Jack's shirt-sleeved arms without being able to do so much as wriggle.

"Oi!" I said. "Put me down!"

"Anything to oblige," said Jack, and threw me in.

If I'd had any idea what he was really doing, I would never have done it. But I was furious and determined that if I was going to be sopping wet, so was he—in all his carefully pressed glory. I seized his arm in one hand, clawing at his cravat in the other, and pulled him into the water with me.

I knew straight away that it was the wrong thing to have done. Jack cannoned into me, his face for the first time utterly and completely surprised, and we flew through a substance that wasn't water or air until we couldn't breathe and our heads cleared the surface of a swiftly running creek. I paddled for the bank, pleasantly surprised at how easy it was to swim with my backpack. It was only when Jack boosted me up and out of the water, and the full weight of it bore down on me, that I realised he had been supporting me the whole time. That annoyed me, so I pointedly turned to help him out of the water instead of leaving him to scrabble out in all the mud as I would have preferred to do.

When we made it to the grass, each of us as muddy as the other, Jack looked around at the grass, the trees, and then the sky. "Ye gods, Mab!" he said. "What have you gotten me into *now*?"

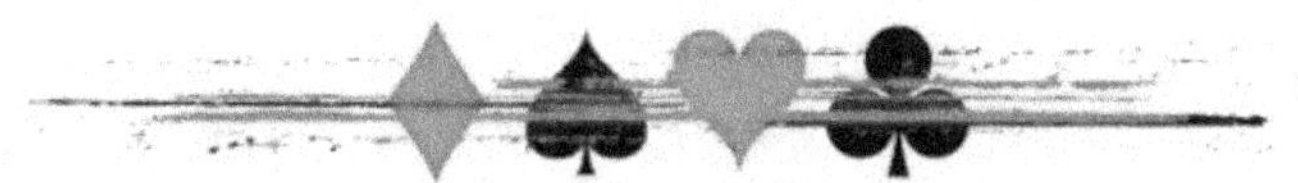

7

Jack ended up staying with me for two weeks. At first, we tried to get him back into Underland by having him jump back into the creek, but as much as that amused me, it did no practical good. At last, Jack, sopping wet and icily annoyed, refused to try again. As he explained it, him coming through to my world was very close to being Against The Rules, and barely possible. When I protested that *I* had brought *him* there, he only said: "Yes, but even if it's not against the rules, she can still make things difficult for me. She's obviously trying to teach me a lesson."

Fortunately, my foster family at that time was a lovely one, and they were happy to invite Jack in when we told them he was my cousin from Sydney. I did finally manage to send him back into Underland through a particularly inviting puddle, but it was as though a door that had been rusty and unwilling to budge was now oiled and gradually widening. I saw Jack more often in mirrors and reflections, and even his presence in puddles began to grow. I still made faces at him, but during those two weeks we had become cautiously used to each other, even if we didn't particularly like each other; and if it hadn't been for the Queen, I would probably have taken down all my mirror-covers except the bathroom one.

8

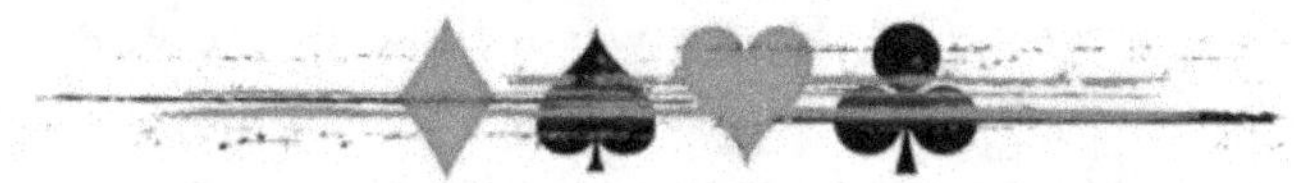

After that, Jack came back every birthday. Sometimes it was just to toss a wrapped gift at me and vanish again. Sometimes it was to pull me into Underland with him and show me somewhere I'd never seen before. And sometimes it was to spend a week or two wherever I happened to be living at the time. It always began the same way: a card on my pillow, no matter where I happened to be living at the time, and then Jack pushing aside the sheet, towel, or curtain that covered the most convenient reflective surface. I got used to him, arrogant, selfish, and annoying as he was. I still saw Hatter and Hare in the ripples and reflections quite often—could call them up in any reflective surface now—and somehow the real world and Australia began to feel less real, and my unreal world of Underland began to feel somehow *more* real. From my twelfth to my eighteenth birthday I spent more time in Underland than out of it, my foster homes changing with such regularity that at last they spoke of keeping me in the group home years earlier than normal. I couldn't blame them—they thought I was running away. Maybe I was. I don't know. All I knew was that, despite the darkness and the feeling of storms gathering that grew thicker

63

the older I became, Underland felt more like home than anywhere I'd ever lived.

When I was with Hatter and Hare, or Sir Blanc, we were always far away from the Queen. She was never really far distant, though. There was always the feeling that she could appear at any time, with her card sharks and casual violence, and cut off someone else's hand. When I was with Jack it was more complicated. The Queen was technically closer—sometimes even on the same floor—but Jack was always a buffer between us. I was never quite sure whether she knew I was there or not, and I didn't really want to know. I was afraid that she did know, and that it was all a part of her plan for me to be there. And some days I was afraid she didn't know, and that when she found out she would kill me and stuff me and put me in her curio room just like she had done with Sir Blanc's wits. Me, stuffed and under glass. Jack singing outside. It didn't stop me going there, though: nothing did. My file at the assessor's office began to grow fat with reports that said things like: *Mabel is bright but disengaged; Mabel does not connect well with the people in her life;* and *Mabel's continued truancy at school and disinclination to interact with the other children is severely hampering both her grades and her ability to settle into the school.* It wasn't long before they sent me to the school counsellor's office; after that, the state counsellor; and when that failed, a psychologist. I briefly considered telling them about Underland—really give them something to take notes about!—but I had the feeling that it would be much harder to sneak away from a mental hospital and I didn't like the idea of being locked up. They probably wouldn't let me put covers over the mirrors there, either.

I did try to be more careful about how long I spent in Underland at a time. A day here, a weekend there. I didn't always visit Hatter and Hare, nor did I always wait for a card on my pillow that meant I'd been invited. I simply packed my backpack—it was pretty battered by now, but it still held all my stuff—and splashed through the nearest puddle. Sometimes I found myself in a garden where the flowers were as supercilious as they were beautiful, their charming tones a constant stream of rude advice on how to do my hair and remarks on my desperate need for mascara. Sometimes I was back in the Chessboard Woods, though I didn't find Sir Blanc there again—I got the impression he was up to Important Business, and perhaps doing something rebellious. Hatter and Hare, when I visited them, wouldn't talk about him; and the one time that I met with him again he was far from his old, cheerful, slightly silly self. It was stupid, of course: Sir Blanc with his wits was *back* to his old self. But I hadn't known him when he had his wits—tired, sad, sharp-eyed and close-mouthed—and I was inclined to regret the change. He wouldn't talk about the Important Business, and the word 'Rebellion' never again crossed his lips, but I knew he was up to something, and Underland itself was changing around me.

9

By the time I was fifteen, there was no doubt about the change. I did more puddle-gazing than travelling, trying to keep under the radar at school and each current foster home, and what I saw in the reflections worried me. When I *did* go to Underland, I mostly visited Hatter and Hare. Though they didn't encourage me to do it, they listened when I told them what I'd seen—the latest outrage or *fracas*, or the Queen's sinister antics in the Mirror Hall—and they didn't tell me not to poke my nose where it wasn't wanted. As far as I understood them, they found my information useful, but didn't want to push me to get it. They never said so, but I knew they were trying to keep me safe as much as they could. By now they didn't question and even seemed to expect my constant presence in Underland: it was an attitude that most Underlanders took to me. I'd thought that my coerced engagement to Jack would have been enough to see me blackballed all over Underland, but to my surprise, I found that no matter where I went in Underland, everyone knew my name. More than that, they knew *of* me. People knew of my first journey to Underland. They knew I'd saved Hatter and Hare from the Jabberwock. It was a topic of dinner-time importance to decide which teapot I had popped out of in my second journey to Underland, and the rescue of Sir Blanc's stolen wits was a story that was told to young Underlanders everywhere. I knew this because in my trawling of the ripples I had often discovered myself to be the topic of discussion. More worrying was the edge I felt in the conversations: it was expectancy and tightly-repressed excitement. I tried to tell myself it was just the slight madness that everyone in Underland had, but I didn't really believe it. It left me a little bit cold, and wondering what it was they expected me to do.

I may have done more puddle-gazing than travelling into Underworld, but I did enough popping in and out of puddles to hone my skills considerably. I was old enough now not just to pop in and out of Underland, but to wonder how it was done and what I could do to make it more seamless. Before long I was slipping into Underland with barely a pause between leap and landing, and arriving within a metre or so of where I expected to be. I also began to make notes and draw maps, which I found more difficult than I expected: Underland's geography occasionally shifted without notice. This made mapping slightly difficult, but was the cause of a useful development: it wasn't long before I learned not just to move between Australia and Underland, but between *here* and *there* in Underland.

The first time I tried to slip between places in Underland was more of an accident than an experiment. I'd been frustrated several times in my journeyings into Underland to find that I had appeared in the wrong place because another bit of it had shifted, and I'd already wondered if it was possible to travel by reflection in Underland. I was watching the ripples in the swimming pool this time: my current foster family was surprisingly rich, and my favourite thing about their house was the pool. By that time I had mapped most of the further reaches of Underland and was beginning to narrow my sights on the centre—the Heart Castle.

That day, I found myself snooping on the Castle itself. I was less frightened of seeing the Queen these days: I'd found that if I avoided gazing at smooth reflective surfaces and stuck to the rough, rippled ones, she wasn't able to see me. That struck me as very useful, and I had been exploiting it for some weeks now in my search for information. I started with Downstairs, where the servants were hunched, hurried, and frightened. Now that I knew how to hear as well as *see*, it was a much more useful exercise. There was always someone saying something interesting around the castle's environs.

There was a difference this time. Downstairs was always dingy and dull when I saw it through the ripples, but it was more than that, now. The servants didn't look at each other. If they passed in the hall or on the stairs, they averted their faces and hunched their shoulders. The kitchen was a fiery, sullen, clanking place without the babble of conversation that should have attended the staff dinner table; but despite the uncomfortable atmosphere, no one seemed willing to take their food and eat elsewhere. It wasn't until I saw the empty places that I realised why. They had been deliberately left empty: plates set at each and cutlery laid beside each setting. I'd heard Hatter and Hare mention a series of three executions that had taken place over the last few weeks—Underlanders who had colluded in the slowly growing rebellion against the Queen. Exactly what they'd done, I'd never been told; but though they also wouldn't tell me what had happened, I knew each of the servants had had their heads cut off, and their families thrown in the Queen's dungeons. Hatter had said: "Big ears in the Castle. That's the problem. Big ears. When people had ears of a decent size, we didn't have these problems," by which I understood that someone had not been careful enough in their talking, and had been overheard by someone loyal to the Queen. It occurred to me that the whole of the Downstairs staff were afraid of each other. The idea made me cautiously hopeful: that there was an informant in the Downstairs staff wasn't ideal, but the general air of suspicion and discomfort also meant that most of the staff were not loyal to the Queen. I made a mental note to mention it to Hatter.

I gazed once more at the empty place settings—that was a kind of silent rebellion in itself—and moved my attention higher in the castle. I found the Queen almost immediately: she was by an open window that overlooked the garden, resplendent in her usual red velvet and white-draped golden head-dress. She reclined grandly in a quilted window seat with shiny red buttons, idly playing with her hand-mirror. It seemed an unusually sedentary position for her, and it wasn't until I pulled back a little that I saw why. There was a painter with an easel sitting across from her, his paintbrush working in sure, certain strokes to create the sweep of the Queen's white veiling. He seemed quite comfortable, but I saw the way her eyes flicked from the painter to the easel and back again, and I wasn't at all surprised when she rose and stole quietly across the carpeted floor toward him. The painter's fingers stiffened, but he kept painting as she leaned over his shoulder. Before long I saw his hands begin to shake slightly, and *still* she was gazing at the painting, her eyes narrow.

At last, in the pleasantest of voices, the Queen said: "Wrong colour."

"I—pardon, your majesty?"

"Wrong colour. Surely you can see the roses are red."

The painter looked out the window, visibly swallowed, and looked back at the Queen.

"*Red*, your majesty?" I could see the roses as well as he could: their petals were pure white.

"Indeed," said the Queen. "Red. They have always been red. Do you dispute it?"

"I—no, your majesty."

"Is that so?" The Queen's voice was growing steadily softer and silkier, and I felt the stirring of fear in my stomach. "Then can you tell me why you thought it good to *paint...them...white*? Do you make a mockery of me?"

"No, your majesty! Pardon me, I beg you!"

"It strikes me that a painter who cannot mix his paints correctly is of little use. What say you to that?"

I could see the painter's eyes. They were wild and scared and horribly unsure. He didn't know what to say. I knew better than him: I knew that whatever he said, it would be the wrong thing. She was bored, and when she was bored there would be blood.

"Really?" said the Queen, as if he'd spoken. "I'm sure you're right. I have some skill in mixing paints myself. Allow me to instruct you. Number Six!"

It all happened so quickly that I wasn't sure which of us realised what happened first, the painter or me. A card shark stepped forward, his sharp nose scenting pain, and at a signal from the Queen he spread the painter's hand wide on his palette. I didn't see where it came from, but suddenly there was a flash of silver blade, and the Queen slashed off the painter's pinky finger. It dropped to the floor, flinging blood as it fell, and the painter simply stared at it, his mutilated hand forgotten on the palette. He made a peculiar noise in his throat—it wasn't very loud, but it made the Queen smile—and then stood mute as she held his injured hand over the blob of white paint on the palette. Crimson dropped into white, leaving tiny divots of red and overflowing into the other colours.

The Queen said, "I believe you mix it now."

He picked up his brush again, face white, and rhythmically worked the crimson through the paint until it was pink—then as crimson as his blood. Then he dabbed it lightly on the edge of his palette and raised his hand to the painting again, stiffly brushing over one of the white roses until it was red. When he was done with that one, he went onto the next.

She wasn't done with him. I could see that. But she let him keep painting and bleeding, mixing the paint with his blood. She sat back in the quilted window seat, her eyes on her tiny hand-held mirror and very nearly closed until suddenly they weren't anymore.

"How delightful," she said. "I see you have two daughters. Pilar and Cat, I believe?"

"My only family, your majesty," said the painter, and I wasn't sure if he was saying it or pleading it.

"They're very fond of pink," said the Queen. I saw the flash of light on her mirror as she turned it enough for the painter to see what she was looking at. She was observing a bedroom from the dressing mirror, where two little girls in identical pink dresses were leaping on a bed that was as offensively pink as their dresses. I heard their squeals of delight as they played, and looked away from the mirror just in time to see the Queen smile again. It wasn't a nice smile.

"Very," said the painter in something of a gasp; and I froze, because the queen was reaching into her mirror. Her fingers touched the glass for the briefest of moments, then sank right through like they had done when I reached through the ripples to save Hatter and Hare. I saw her pinch and release, then one of the little girls hurtled from the bed and hit the floor with a crash. The painter cried out, but after a stunned moment his little girl picked herself up, briefly crinkling her chin in pain, and climbed back onto the bed with her sister.

"Little children bounce so well, don't they?" said the Queen. She smiled at the painter and went back to her mirror. With her eyes on it, she said, softly and coldly, "You may continue painting."

He went back to painting—what else could he do? The Queen, meanwhile, watched her little mirror and smiled. I hoped she'd had her fun, but after a few minutes of trembling brushstrokes from the painter, she called: "Number Five!" The painter started horribly, and while he desperately tried to fix the smudge he'd made, the Queen said: "Number Five, this ah, talented and hardworking artist has two little girls. Bring them to me."

The painter made another involuntary slash of crimson across the canvas and stumbled away from his easel. "Your majesty, I *beg* you–!"

"Return to your painting," said the Queen, with a terrible coldness in her voice. The Number Five card shark was gone in a flash, his eyes glistening with bloodthirsty joy, and the painter stood trembling by his easel.

I almost stepped straight through the ripples to the painter's —and my own—doom. But there was a chilling anger eating away at the hot fury, and it told me to wait. Having waited for that essential moment, it occurred to me that it was no use going to the painter's help, only to be caught myself. I saw him taken away by two more card sharks as he tried to dash from the room, his paints thrown aside, and knew I couldn't help him. Not now. But I *could* snatch his little girls away before they went through the same thing I had gone through as a child. It wasn't likely that they would be as lucky as I'd been. So instead of leaping into Underland in the fierceness of my anger, I deliberately pushed away the scene I had been observing, and searched for card shark Number Five. I caught up with him in the outer court of the castle: he wasn't taking one of the covered chairs—which wasn't unusual for a card shark—but he also didn't bother with a horse or a hackney. That meant he wasn't going far. I kept my rippled view following along behind him until he turned into one of the flower-named streets closest to the Heart Castle. He stopped at the fourth house in the street, one that wasn't very grand but was well kept, and set the knocker echoing across the street. I didn't waste another moment. I found a reflection in the house, hoping it wasn't a flat reflection that the Queen would be able to see, and stepped through.

I came out, gasping, in a small decorative pool in the painter's marbled hall. Behind me, I heard footsteps echoing, and looked over my shoulder to see a servant heading for the front door. It was too late to save him: he was already opening the door as I splashed out of the pool. So I left him to die, a dry sob of fear and sorrow in my throat, and ran as fast as I could up the wide stairs that must lead to the family rooms upstairs. I tried not to listen to the noise behind me, but I heard the sound of a struggle, the servant screaming, and the thump of a body when it hit the marble floor. Then there were the soft, slapping sounds of Number Five's wide feet as he crossed the hall. I didn't know if he'd seen me or not, but it didn't really matter. He wouldn't hurry himself: he would continue at the same steady, determined pace until he caught up with me or the painter's daughters, whoever came first. I took the stairs two at a time, and was still fumblingly checking doors when I heard Number Five's tread on the bottom stair. The next door I tried led into the small suite I'd seen through the Queen's mirror, and I stared at it wildly for a moment, finding it empty of children despite the toys carelessly left on the floor and the two girl's coats lying in a puddle on the floor.

"Doors!" I panted, with a fizz of inspiration. I snatched at the big key that hung by a pink thread beside the door and darted back out to sprint from door to door, locking each one. I only had time to lock the first four doors before I had dive for the girls' suite again, slamming the door and locking it behind me.

There! I thought in satisfaction. Let him try and figure out which one it was! He would be naturally suspicious of the locked doors, and perhaps that would buy me some time to find the girls. Stepping lightly, I checked the other rooms in the suite, from the bathing room to the closet stuffed with pink skirts and big straw hats. I was crossing the room again to check under the bed when I heard Number Five break down the first of the doors in a terrifyingly loud splintering of wood. My head snapped around even though I'd been expecting it, and I caught sight of a flutter of pink in the window. I abandoned the bed immediately, and leaned out the window with my heart thumping loudly.

The girls were playing by a fountain in the garden below, floating paper boats peopled with flower petals, their hats bowling along the lawn behind them in a brisk breeze. I heard a rattle and a snap-snap of noise: Number Five must have also seen the girls, and his head was protruding from a window to my left. He saw me at the same time that I saw him, and his teeth gnashed at me. I couldn't tell if it was in warning or promise, but either way, he seemed to be enjoying himself. I began to scramble out the window, but he was quicker than I; and when he was out, he threw himself from the window with the kind of careless abandon that was only explained by the light way in which he fluttered to the lawn. He looked back up at me, with my one leg out of the window and my mouth open, and this time there was no doubting his malicious glee. He was closer to the girls: he knew it, and there was nothing I could do about it.

So I did something about it anyway. I pulled my leg back through the window and hauled the window frame back down. It slammed down on the sill and my reflection shuddered at me for a wobbly moment before I pushed cleanly through the window and emerged, wet and shivering, in the fountain. The little girls were both screaming when I rose from the water. They weren't screaming at me: they had seen the card shark approaching them, and they knew he was there for them. I wrapped my dripping arms around them from behind, which prompted more screaming and quite a bit of determined wriggling, but I pulled them back into the water with me without knowing exactly where I was going. A moment later we tumbled out of a bedroom mirror onto plush black carpet, dampening the threads around us. By the time we were rolling across the carpet, my arms around the both of them, the girls had stopped screaming and were clinging to me instead, their eyes wide and unsure. Dazed and dizzy, I looked around me incredulously. How on earth had I managed to come out in Jack's suite? We were in his closet: a vast, many-racked room with three dressing mirrors and rail upon rail of clothing. There were his shoes, too, pointy-toed and shiny: pair after pair of the things. I felt a momentary twinge of annoyance despite our peril: why should one boy own so many shoes?

I didn't dare leave the girls in Jack's closet: not after coming through a mirror. I threw three of his elegant, tailed suit jackets over the mirrors and carried the girls off with me into the bathroom. They didn't struggle. I think they may have been crying, but I couldn't stop to soothe their tears when things could get a lot worse than tears if we were caught. I pulled up short in the bathroom, surprised and suspicious to find that there was already water in the bathtub. And as it had been the last time I was here, every mirror in the room had been covered. It almost looked like my bathroom back in Australia.

To stop the little girls being frightened again, I said to them: "We're going to jump through again, okay? I promise the card shark won't get you."

One of them wiped her nose on my sleeve, but the other said: "N'yep," and though I wasn't sure whether that was a yes or a no, at least they didn't scream again when I stepped carefully into the tub.

We came out in a freshly washed stew pot in the Queen's kitchen, exploding in a clatter of lid against the lip of the pot and tumbling to the floor. It was fortunate that we'd landed in this one and not the one at present simmering stew over the fire. Our clattering and the whimpering of the little girls prompted a shuffling of feet and several Underland swear words somewhere in one of the corners. I looked around to find a couple of castle servants gaping at us, dismay in their eyes.

"You shouldn't be here," said the girl, her voice hushed. She was looking at me with recognition in her eyes. "She won't like it. We've already lost three men."

"I know," I said quietly. "But she's cut off one of the painter's fingers and she sent a card shark for his little girls. I had to do *something*."

They both looked at me with wide eyes and open mouths. At last, the boy closed his mouth and reformed it to ask: "You went up against a card shark to get them? Does the Queen know?"

"Not yet. I need–"

"Yes," said the girl, simply.

"But you don't know–"

"Yes," said the boy. "It doesn't matter."

"What about the men who were lost?"

The boy's face darkened. "That was something different," he said. "That was...someone didn't like what we were talking about and told the Queen. We still don't know who it was."

"If you talked anywhere that had a mirror, it probably wasn't anyone," I said, remembering the flashes of heart red that I'd seen sometimes when I saw the Downstairs staff. Even if the Queen hadn't had her Mirror Hall, she would still have been able to see them in her hand-held mirror.

"Never near a mirror," said the girl. "We know better."

"What about flat reflecting surfaces? Windows?"

There was a sick look in their eyes. "She can see us through *windows* now?"

"Probably always could," I said, with difficulty. The flame that had flared in their eyes was dying into the same kind of dead acceptance I had seen in the eyes of the rest of the Downstairs staff. "The kitchen's safe. It's just glass that seems to work for her. And even then, if it's not flat, she doesn't seem to be able to see through."

The boy drew in a deep breath through his teeth, and I saw the girl's eyes flicking toward him, lighting with speculation and determination.

"What do you need us to do?" he asked. "She'll have him in the dungeon by now. We heard someone being taken down there a little while ago."

"Take the girls out of the castle. Find somewhere with water, and I'll come and get you when the others are safe."

They nodded in tandem, each of them taking a small, frightened girl from me.

I said: "I'm going to get Jack. He'll help." They didn't look convinced, so I added: "And get ready to take all the staff out of the castle: we're going to break out *everyone* from the dungeons."

I'm still not sure why I did it, but I went back to Jack's room. Maybe I thought that if he could just understand what was going on outside his velveted and satined world, he would fight back. He would see the injustices as I did—he *had* to—and if anyone could do something about the Queen, it was Jack. Maybe there was a part of me that just wanted to see if he would help me if it involved any risk at all for himself. I couldn't recall a time he'd actually done so. He'd helped me once or twice, but it had never been in such a way as to leave himself without any way of turning it into an innocent action on his own part if it went badly. I wanted to know if he would do the right thing when it came right down to it. With the darkness spreading over

Underland, it seemed to me that there would soon come a time when even Jack would have to choose sides, rules or not. So when I left the kitchen, I dipped only slightly back into the ripples and climbed out of the bathtub in Jack's suite. I stepped out onto the cool, black and white tiles, drying swiftly, and padded softly into the main room to wait for him.

He was already there—stretched out on one of the black sofas, his crossed ankles propped against the sofa back and his fingers linked beneath his head. His eyes were on me before I noticed him: he must have been waiting for me. I checked myself, then kept walking anyway. I should have expected it.

"I thought you were back," said Jack, flicking his legs down. "Mab, must you use my best suit coats to cover the mirrors? They're hand sewn and embroidered."

"Did you leave the bath full of water for me?"

"Do you know, I'm almost certain that thinking everything is about oneself is the first sign of madness."

I didn't mean to smile but I think I must have, because he smiled back at me with nothing arrogant or sarcastic about it. I said: "Thanks."

"I have no idea what you're talking about," said Jack, but the left side of his lips still curved up just slightly. "Be careful Mab, you'll only confuse me by being pleasant."

"Don't worry, I haven't come to be pleasant."

"Perhaps I'm pessimistic, but I don't believe I was ever under that impression," said Jack, rising from his sofa. "Sit down."

"I was Downstairs earlier," I said, watching him. He seemed to be unpacking a small cabinet that had liquid-filled bottles and glass swizzle-sticks in it. He took out three of the bottles and two small glasses, and mixed something that fizzed and bubbled, and scented the air with the sweet, sharp smell of mulberries.

"More of your revolutionary little friends, I suppose," said

Jack, but his voice was pleasant enough. I had an idea that he was trying not to quarrel with me, and it left me feeling uneasy. I didn't know whether to take pains to be polite, or to be rude on principle.

I said: "Not exactly. Well, if they weren't before, I'll bet they are now, anyway."

Jack narrowed his eyes at me from across the room, and scooped up the two full glasses. "Have you been annoying Mother Dearest again?"

"Probably. She cut off a painter's finger this morning, did you know?"

"Yes, she likes playing with her food," said Jack. "You shouldn't have got involved."

"She sent a card shark after his kids, Jack. What was I supposed to do?"

"Tell your revolutionary little friends. Keep out of it. Hope someone else helps."

"There was no time, and no one would have helped."

"Then I don't see why you did. If Underlanders are ignoring Underlanders, I don't see why an otherworld girl should be risking her neck."

"It's not like that!" I flashed. I wasn't sure which offended me more: his judgement of Underlanders, or his casual exclusion of myself from Underland. "They're scared! The streets are bare and everyone is hiding behind their doors and shutters. Have you *been* outside the castle in the last four years?"

"Why should I?" said Jack coolly. "It's cool and peaceful in here. Out there it's all madness and fighting and harsh things."

"What, like the truth?"

"Don't sneer, Mab," he said, strolling back to his seat with both drinks. "It's rude. Have a drink."

I didn't want a drink, but he'd already made it so I took it anyway. It was something sherbetty and lovely, and after a little while I forgot I hadn't wanted it. Jack sat back down and crossed one leg over the other. He looked elegant and rich and ridiculously poised.

"Well, then," he said. "This is just delightful. To what do I owe this pleasure?"

I couldn't tell whether he was being ironic or not, so I ignored his question. Instead, I said: "You need to come Downstairs with me. We have to help someone."

Jack raised one elegant brow. "I'll do nothing of the kind. Downstairs is no place for me to be wandering around: it's far too dirty. If it comes to that, it's no place for you to be wandering around, either. The Prince's fiancée shouldn't be consorting with the staff."

"I am *not* your fiancée," I said. "I told you. I'm not old enough to be engaged."

"Sorry," said Jack, shrugging. "It's done. You can't help it, *I* can't help it: it's all very boring arguing about it. It might be less boring when you're older."

"And I also refuse to be engaged to a selfish little rich boy," I added, looking around me in disgust. "Do you know what it's like Downstairs?"

Jack sighed. "Don't be so earnest and severe, Mab. Downstairs is where the servants live. Of course it's going to be drab."

"It's not just drab, the people there are scared, too. She's doing horrible things to them, and they all know they could be next."

"This is Underland. Everybody is scared. It's simply a matter of making sure more people are scared of you than *vice versa*."

"Oh, is that what you've been doing?" I didn't even try to disguise the disgust in my voice. "Making sure people are scared of you?"

"In a manner of speaking," said Jack, his eyes avoiding mine. "Mother Dearest is, anyway. I'm just along for the ride."

"Sometimes," I said meditatively, "Sometimes I start to think you're not so bad. And then you say something that reminds me what snivelling little dirtbag you are."

There was a moment of silence before Jack cleared his throat and said: "You've a sharp little tongue on you, Mab."

"Well, maybe you shouldn't be a snivelling little dirtbag. Maybe I'd be nicer."

"Why should I care if you're nicer?" said Jack swiftly. His face was a little whiter than usual.

"Heck if I know. You know what I do know? I don't like you. Actually, the more I get to know you, the less I like you. You–"

"All right!" Jack said, lunging to his feet with a slash of bright red in each cheek. "All right, Mab! I've grasped your meaning! You needn't belabour it!"

My drink seemed to have lost its flavour. I put it down with a grimace and said: "Enjoy your pretty little rooms. I have to go back Downstairs."

"A pleasure, as always," said Jack, with something of a bite to his voice. That was new and strange, because as objectionable as Jack was, he usually had his temper well under control. He opened the door for me anyway, with something of a hasty hand, and closed it behind me with more than a snap. I was left to creep back Downstairs again as best I might, feeling cold and oddly abandoned. It had been stupid to expect Jack to do anything: he always had been selfish.

I was at something of a loss when I got back Downstairs, but the girl—Reena—was still waiting for me and I couldn't disappoint her. I said: "Jack couldn't come," because I found myself ashamed to confess that Jack had outright refused to help. It shouldn't have, but it somehow felt as if his selfishness reflected on me. "I've got another way of getting into the dungeons, though. Are the girls safe?"

"Penrod has them," said Reena. My news of Jack didn't seem

to surprise her. She looked frightened—or was she excited? It was hard to tell with the glitter in her eyes and the determined set to her chin. "All the rest of the staff are ready to leave, too: we're going to clear this place out. Penrod says we'll meet in the Chessboard Woods."

"All right," I said. "Because we're going to clear out the dungeons, and if there's anyone left here–"

"There won't be," said Reena; and her chin was even more determined than before. "What do you need me to do? Can I come with you?"

"If you like. It'll be dangerous, though."

"*Breathing's* dangerous now," Reena said grimly. "What do you need me to do?"

"How do they feed the prisoners?"

"Um, well, there's a galley down there. The food goes straight from the galley to the cells."

"Are there guards near the galley?"

"Yes. Well, no. There are about four locked gates between here and there, guards at each. The galley has a guard at its outer door, but its inner door opens straight into the cells' common area."

"Is there any other way in?"

Reena nodded. "The main entrance. But you have to go through the other four gates to get to that one anyway."

"Is it bars, or solid?"

She had to think about that one a bit longer. At last, slowly, she said: "I *think* it's solid."

"If we can get in, will there be anyone already there?"

"No. They only let in cook, and only once a day: for break-fast. How are you—oh! The pots?"

"Yes," I said, more confidently than I felt. "Do you still want to come along?"

"Yes," she said; and I wondered if *she* was pretending to be braver than she felt. "When do we start?"

"Now," I said. I reached out to our distended reflection in the huge curve of a nearby wok, seeing the flash of another reflection behind that, and pulled us both through the curve and into the prison galley.

Reena's fingers were digging painfully into my arm when we stumbled out into an avalanche of dirty potatoes. Something *clanged* behind us as a potato ricocheted off it, and I threw a brief look over my shoulder. This time we'd come through a small ironwork stove. There was no real chimney, which explained the soot on the ceiling and the lingering scent of scorched *everything*. The Queen obviously didn't like the idea of anyone creeping up or down the chimney. I doubted we'd find any ice vents, either.

"I didn't feel anything," said Reena. She sounded slightly disgruntled, and I grinned.

"I didn't the first time, either," I told her. "I only started noticing when I started going through by myself. Here, help me fill the potato bin with water."

Reena looked surprised, but helped me with the wooden barrel. We tipped the rest of the potatoes all over the floor and put it below the pump, where Reena's practised pumping saw an outpouring of cold water quickly fill it. It was much harder to move it once it was full, but between the two of us we managed to rock it from the galley to the cells.

A buzz of conversation started up straight away: Reena and I were too busy moving the barrel to pay attention, but from the corner of my eyes I saw prisoners shifting between the open, inner doors of the barred cells. When we finally wrestled it into place by the left-hand run of cells, all of the prisoners had gathered around the bars near us. The painter was there, his missing finger bandaged with a frilly bit of material that had to have come from the sleeve of the woman standing next to him. I didn't recognise any of the others, but when I ran my eyes over the cells on the right side, I caught sight of a white grin in the darkness.

"Cat Cheshire!" I said, frowning. He had been friendly with Jack: how had he ended up here? "What happened to you?"

The grin moved into the foreground, bringing with it Cat Cheshire's now rather battered hat and his dark glasses. The rest of him looked as battered as his hat, but he still had his swagger.

"I was playing games with the Queen."

"Cheated, did you?"

"Baby, don't be like that," drawled Cat Cheshire. "Naw, she was the better player. Outdid me at the game and outmaneuvered me at the run."

"Why didn't Jack get you out of here?"

"You don't know Jack too well, baby. Are *you* here to break me out?"

"You and them both," I said, and upturned the barrelful of water.

It surged across the floor in a dirty, tsunami of possibility, and each of the captive Underlanders moved back to avoid wetting their feet. That made me smile a bit: they'd be happy enough to get their feet wet once they knew this puddle was their way out. I slid smoothly into the puddle and back out again, this time on the other side. The Underlanders alternately hissed in surprise and gasped in delight when I appeared among them.

"Right," I said: "Two at a time. Everyone line up."

They did line up. Quickly and quietly, and entirely trustfully. I put my arms around the first two of them and drew them into the puddle with me. This time I didn't bring us out back in the main prison: I went deeper into the puddle and surfaced in the Chessboard Woods. It was quite some time since I had first seen

Sir Blanc, but the woods didn't seem to have changed at all. I hoped fervently that the red knight was still stuck in his tree and unable to joust at passing strangers.

"Don't change squares until you're all here," I said, just in case; and slipped back into my pool for the next two Underlanders. They were waiting for me, their eyes bright and frighteningly hopeful, and when I appeared again their eyes brightened still further. I tried to ignore it, but it was hard to ignore so much determined adulation. It made me feel uncomfortable and slightly dishonest: really, I hadn't done *that* much more than Jack.

It took longer than I liked to get them all out. Even before I turned to the cell on the right side of the prison I'd been at it for the better part of an hour, ferrying two people at a time through to the Chessboard Woods. I didn't like to take more than two at a time because I wasn't sure where they would end up if I lost one of them between surfaces. Still, it made me smile to think that tonight Jack would have to fetch his own supper. The idea, as funny as it was, reminded me that the Queen would also have to fetch her own supper, and that thought wasn't quite so funny. I hoped the Chessboard Woods was far enough away from her ire. I was reasonably certain that she couldn't travel the way I did, so any chase she gave would have to be via shark-drawn carriage. That would give everyone a chance to move on and find somewhere safe to hide: prisoners and castle staff alike.

The painter and his lady friend were among the last to be taken: I think they might have planned it, because when we were the last three in the cell he grasped my arm to stop me stepping into the puddle. "Thank you," he said. "We'll try to make it count."

Count for what, exactly? I wondered, as I took them through the puddle to safely. The rebellion was far away and spoken of in whispers. It wasn't here and now. But these people, these ordinary people, were talking like it was here and now.

When we were in the Chessboard Woods, I said: "I'll bring your girls once the others are out," because I didn't know what else to say. "Wait for the castle staff: they'll be here within two days."

The painter hugged me, a fierce, rough hug that left blood on my shirt and tears in his eyes, and I slipped back to the cells before anyone else could do the same. Things in Underland were becoming all too real, and I found that it was hard to endure the looks that were bearing down on me. They were too heavy—heavy with meaning, heavy with hope, heavy with expectation—and I was eager to get away from them.

They wanted me to stay, after. I don't know why I didn't expect that—or why I didn't stay, for that matter. Maybe I didn't feel old enough for the responsibility. Maybe it was just nice being able to drop in and help, and then leave again. Maybe I was scared. Whatever the reason, I left as soon as the last Underlander was safely in the Chessboard Woods; without saying goodbye, without fanfare, and most of all without tears.

10

I didn't leave entirely unnoticed: Cat Cheshire came with me when I went home. Nowhere in Underland was safe for him to play, he said, and if he couldn't play he didn't want to do anything. I told him bluntly that if he didn't play for money and wouldn't work for it, he would be doing something whether or not he wanted to—starving.

"That's why I'm coming with you," he said. "Jack did try to warn me before it happened. He told me there are places I can earn a good living in your world."

"You could earn a good living in any world," I said, as blunt in my praise as I had been in my dissent. Cat Cheshire's skill on the piano was something Australia hadn't heard since the 1940s.

I had no one to introduce him to and only a small amount of useful advice, but Cat Cheshire was the sort who tended to land on his feet. He got himself a job playing nights at an old '40s style club, and the next I heard of him, he was touring the world. He had taken to my world with as much verve and considerably more success than I had taken to his. Forsaking what was behind, he had seized on what was ahead, and it seemed to me that perhaps I would be facing the same decision before too many more years.

I didn't see Jack for three years after that. To tell the truth, I wasn't sorry for it. I didn't want to be fond of someone as horrible as Jack, and it seemed to me that we had gotten so used to each other over the years that I *had* very nearly become fond of him. There were still the birthday presents every year and I still saw Jack in the reflections, but the visiting stopped: both mine and his. And I suppose I really had been visiting him, if it came to that. It was Jack I visited most often when I went into Underland—Jack I was most likely to see. That all came to an end; though I still visited Underland, and I still experimented with my puddle-jumping. It wasn't Underland I wanted to give up: just Jack.

When I was eighteen, I came back to find the tea-table broken, the teacups scattered and the cutlery strewn through the forest. The only sign of the Hatter was his multifaceted hat, crushed and forsaken by the broken table. I sat down in the grass with the hat cradled in my arms, frightened and unsure of anything but that an evil I had felt threatening had finally arrived. Where was Hatter? Where was the Hare? Hatter wouldn't have willingly left without his hat, I knew.

When I wasn't feeling so cold, I rose with the hat still clutched between my hands, and searched through the tumbled remains of the tea party. The grass had been flattened by sharp, metallic footprints that could only have been formed by card sharks, and on a jagged edge of broken chair I found a clump of red velvet. *The Queen!* Where had she taken Hatter and Hare? And what, I wondered in sudden coldness, did she want with them? I'd always been quite sure that they were involved in something dangerous and tricky: their mad way of speaking was always irritating, hard to follow, and sometimes stunningly to the point, and I had often been surprised by a gleam of intelligence in Hatter's eyes. Even Hare, who hadn't ever shown what I might consider to be intelligence, had often shown a cunning, sideways streak of slyness in his dealings. Had their madness been a cover? No, I didn't think so. I thought it was more a case of them desperately using every advantage in a silent, deadly war against the Queen. Once, long ago, Sir Blanc had spoken of the rebellion I'd seen brewing over the last few years. He hadn't had his wits about him at the time and hadn't been able to tell me anything else about it—nor had Hatter or Hare ever been persuaded or tricked into talking about it—and eventually I'd stopped asking. It was just one more cog in the ticking, whirring, complicated darkness that I felt creeping over Underland from the first time I popped out in the teapot.

Now I wished I'd made more of an effort. Maybe asked Jack. He wouldn't have told me, but I might have been able to trick it out of him. Sometimes he had been relaxed enough to say more than he meant to. In my fear and confusion it took me too long to remember that I still had my own ways of finding things out. All I needed to do was find a source of liquid. What I saw in the ripples would tell me what had happened. In the last three years I had learned a thing or two about the ripples—and more than a thing or two about the Queen, whose skill in the Mirror Hall may have earned her more information about me than I would have liked her to have—and I knew exactly what to do. Hatter, of course, had talked madly of possibilities and probabilities when I first met him: it was only a short step from there to realising that if I was clever about it, I could see more than the present in the ripples. I'd already learned that I could alter things in the ripples—stretch time and space, and make things that Weren't as if they *Were*—and not only did I learn, I improved. It was a talent that had never much helped me in what I was seeing less and less as the 'real' world, but it was very useful in Underland. I had only ever managed to see a few seconds into the future; and even then, I had never actually proved even to myself that it *was* the future. The past was much easier. Like the Hatter had said at the time, it wasn't so much a matter of looking backwards, but Seeing Things Differently. I found myself wondering, as I searched the smashed crockery for any unbroken teacups, exactly how much the Queen could see in her Mirror Hall. I doubted she could see into the past: there were too many people who would have been in her dungeons if she could. That she could make the same kinds of changes I could make in the ripples was certain: I'd seen her do it myself. Now I wondered if it was possible that she saw the future instead.

I searched among the broken porcelain for some time, but none of the cups were whole enough to contain so much as a drop of tea, and all of the teapots had been smashed to smithereens. Even Hatter and Hare's pretty little pond had been drained. The Queen had been incredibly thorough. I put Hatter's hat on my head to keep it out of the general mess, and it wasn't until I dashed it off my head again in frustration that it occurred to me how silly I had been. I'd seen Hatter use the reflective patches on his hat to do much more than provide a pretty head covering. I made a sound of disgust at my own stupidity and sat down on a fragment of chair that remained amidst the general wreckage, setting the hat on my knees. As I looked at it, one of the flashy pieces reflected a scrap of something from some time that wasn't now. I narrowed my eyes on it, hunching over the hat. At first there was only darkness and the sensation of something missing. Then I saw Hatter and Hare at the tea table, Hatter pouring tea into the sugar bowl and gravely stirring the sugary mess with a twig, and Hare thumping the side of the table vigorously with his hind leg. He still had his crutch with him—he had begun carrying it with him when he lost his front paw, despite the fact that he didn't need it in order to get around *and* that it meant his one remaining front paw was occupied. With the crutch he was buttering crumpets and offering them to Hatter. They looked up at the same time—looked right at me, and I thought for a moment that they could see me. Then the reflection...disappeared. Well, not quite *disappeared*. It was more like the reflection suddenly lost sight of Hatter and Hare and was showing me a dark, blank screen instead. I hadn't seen anything like it in my ripples before. I was still frowning at the blank nothingness of it when all of a sudden, there was the tea-table again. Only this time it was smashed to pieces and Hatter and Hare were gone. The scene was abandoned. No, not quite abandoned: I caught a flash of movement at the farthest corner I could discern, and saw...*Jack.* It was Jack! Walking quickly and purposefully away in his red suit and pointy shoes, surrounded by card sharks.

I went straight to the Heart Castle. I was so frightened, or angry, or confused, that I pushed through the card sharks at the castle court and then the grand entrance. I had begun to think that the Queen knew of my visits to Underland—had always known of them—and it seemed only natural that they would let me pass. I was instinctively sure that she wouldn't have me killed: not until she saw me married to Jack, anyway. I didn't know what to expect after that. I didn't even know why she wanted us to marry. But I was certain, that day, that none of the card sharks or guards would stop me: and none of them did. I swept past them, my chin high, and stepped briskly through the halls until I found Jack's suite. This time, when I flung open the door and it cracked against the wall, Jack really *did* jump. But by then I was too pent up with fury and terror to enjoy it. I simply marched up to him, and when he stepped back, a flash of alarm —or was it anticipation?—in his black-flecked eyes, I followed him step for step.

"*What*," I said in a voice that was cold and precise, shoving him in the chest with every word, "*What* have you done with Hatter and Hare?"

"Oh, what a disappointment!" said Jack, forced to sit down unexpectedly on the bed to escape my shoving. "I really expected–"

"What have you done with Hatter and Hare!"

"Mab, I really can't have you assaulting me in this manner. There are other, far more pleasant methods of assault that I can think of off-hand, as a matter of fact; and since I've not seen hide nor hair of you for three years now, I *do* think–"

"*Where are they?*"

"I much prefer to associate with the less subversive elements of Underland, actually," said Jack. "Mother Dearest, on the other hand, almost certainly knows where your mad little friends are if they have disappeared."

"I saw you in the reflections!"

"I'm more than willing to provide you with all the company you desire, Mab. You don't have to watch me in the reflections."

I made a pleasingly realistic choking noise that caused Jack to raise his brows. "Yuck. Why would I watch you in the reflections? I was looking at the old reflections to see what happened, and–"

This time it was Jack who made a particularly realistic choking noise. "You were looking at *what*?"

"The old reflections," I said impatiently. "You know, the ones that show what happened instead of what's really happening."

"Ye gods!" said Jack. "No wonder she's afraid of you! Wait, if you saw what happened, why are you asking me about it? I didn't do it!"

"I couldn't see all of it," I told him grimly. "The reflection went dark and then the picture was gone. When it cleared, *you* were there."

"I see," said Jack thoughtfully. "Mother Dearest is up to her old tricks again. She must know what you can do."

"What do you mean?"

"She's trying to make us distrust each other."

"Why? I already don't like you."

Jack sighed. "Mab, could you at least *attempt* cordiality? She wants us to get married, but she doesn't want us to get too close to each other. We might start planning things."

"I've been planning things for years," I said.

"I'm perfectly well aware of that, thank you!" said Jack. "It's the bad company you keep. Do you honestly think they were looking after you, Mab? The quickest way I know to end up in the dungeons or decorating the castle walls with your head is to be planning things in Underland."

"Hatter and Hare didn't know about it," I told him. I wasn't sure if that was quite true: both Hatter and Hare had been —*were*—very cunning. But as with everything else I did in Underland, though they hadn't encouraged me, they hadn't stopped me, either. "And they don't let me get involved."

"Wonderful job they've been doing," said Jack, one of his brows raised.

"You're one to talk! It's your fault I'm in Underland at all!"

For once, Jack looked completely taken aback. "Well really,

Mab! To be blaming me for Mother Dearest's actions is really beyond the pale! I've enough of my own faults to be owning to, thank you very much!"

"Who did she blood-bond me to?" I said grimly. "It wasn't Hatter!"

"I really can't be blamed for what my mother does in pursuance of power!" said Jack. "And I refuse to be compared with that mad little muck-raker! I'm *far* better looking, and we won't even get into the issue of style and fashion, thank you very much."

"I like the way Hatter dresses," I told him stiffly. "It's better than your horrible pointy shoes, anyway."

"Mab, I understand that you're angry, but I'll thank you not to mock my choice of apparel! I'll accept aspersions made upon my character, but—actually, no! As a matter of fact, I won't! I refuse to take the blame for something that my mother probably did. She's obviously made it look like I was there, and as much as I admire her skill, I'd like you to know that I *wasn't*."

"How would she do that?" I demanded. I didn't trust Jack, and despite the Queen's way with mirrors, surely she wasn't capable of making reflections show me something that wasn't true. Or was that something she could do in the Mirror Hall, too?

Jack's eyes were on me, and they had a frozen sort of look to them. "You actually think I could have done this," he said at last. "I'd be flattered if I thought you knew what sort of skill it takes to pull off a trick like this."

"So you had *nothing to do* with any of it?" I couldn't help it: my tone made it an accusation.

Jack shrugged. "There are two things in Underland I know of that could do this sort of job. Neither of which, I hasten to add, I am currently in possession."

"Two things?" I looked at him sceptically. "And what are they?"

"I'm reasonably certain that Hatter's hat can do it, and just slightly less sure that you're capable of it."

"I *have* Hatter's hat," I said coldly. "And I'm here, so maybe you can think of something else."

"I never thought I'd be sorry to see you displaying such subtlety, Mab!" said Jack. "I'm not lying, if that's what you're suggesting. As a matter of fact—dear me! Mab, I don't suppose it was the Hatter's hat that you used to look back at what happened, was it?"

I knew in one galling moment what he meant—and what must have happened. I said reluctantly: "I might have."

"It never occurred to you to wonder why Mother Dearest didn't take it with her? Something so valuable and potentially useful?"

I sighed. "She left it behind because it was more valuable to her *here*."

"I imagine so," said Jack. "So very like my dear mother! No doubt she's smiling away to herself at this very moment."

"I don't care if she's smiling," I said. It wasn't true, of course. It was sickening to think how easily the Queen had manipulated me. "I just want to know where Hatter and Hare are."

"Not in the dungeons, at any rate," said Jack. "Mab, I realise that you're determined to play with lawbreakers and rebels, but was there any need to abscond with the cook and the footmen? Have you any idea how badly card sharks cook?"

I grinned for the first time that day. So the loss of all the castle servants at once *had* made an impression! "Serves you right."

"Oh, undoubtedly. But it has put you rather at a disadvantage: once upon a time, Mother Dearest would have merely imprisoned them in the dungeon. You've encouraged her to greater feats of imagination, I'm afraid."

I sobered at once, and I thought Jack winced a little. Was he sorry he'd said it? Why? He'd never shown concern for anyone's feelings before.

"I'll need to use your bathtub," I said.

"As always, it is at your disposal," said Jack. He stood up, which brought me to realise just how adversarially close to him I was, and ushered me toward the bathroom with one arm around my waist.

"I know where it is," I said testily, pulling away. I entered the room ahead of him, and found with a slight feeling of familiarity that the bathtub was still as full as it had been last time. Almost as though it had never been emptied, or as though–

"I still get them to fill it every day," said Jack, his hands in his pockets and his shoulders leaning against the door frame. "I'm not exactly sure why I bother when all you do is attack me whenever I see you. Verbally *and* physically, if it comes to that."

I threw him an impatient look over my shoulder, and he held up both hands in surrender, lapsing into silence as I turned back to the water in the bathtub.

This time when I looked into the ripples, they showed me the truth. The Queen had come upon Hatter and Hare suddenly with her card sharks, bundling them into the carriage with her, and had taken them off to goodness knows where. Since it was a piece of the past, fixed and certain, I couldn't follow them in the ripples when they left. I remained staring at events that had already happened until the card sharks came back, smashing the tea-table and its accoutrements, and deliberately leaving Hatter's hat where I had found it. I dismissed the sight and sat back on the bathroom floor, surprised to find Jack there beside me with his legs very carefully bent to avoid creasing his trousers as much as possible.

"I've only ever seen Mother do that," he said. "Only in the Mirror Hall, however, and never like *that*. She can't get more than a few seconds into the past. I think it must bother her, because she insists upon telling me that one should never look to the past, but to the future."

I huffed a sigh, but it had to be said. "Sorry I thought you were a lying scumbag."

"That's very big of you. Perhaps now you'd care to hear what I have to say?"

I gave him a disbelieving look. "What, you're going to *help* me?"

"I hate to seem a pedant, Mab," said Jack. "But I seem to remember helping you out several times over the years."

"Helping yourself, you mean," I said bluntly. "You only help when you can get something out of it."

Jack's eyes narrowed. "I also seem to remember mentioning that sharp tongue of yours. Do you want help, or do you not? And before you open your mouth again, do remember who it is you're trying to help and consider whether it may not be just as well to be polite."

I opened my mouth to be less than polite; and Jack must have known what was coming, because he grabbed me by the nape of the neck and firmly pushed my face into his suit lapels where my mumbled insults were too muffled to be understood. More irritatingly, he patted my head with his other hand and said: "There, there. I'm sure it'll pass soon. Shh."

When I finally managed to wrench my head free, he was smiling at me in a way that made me want to punch him. Instead of doing that, I drew a breath and said: "All right, then. Help me."

"Amazing. You manage to make even a plea for help sound antagonistic."

"That's because I don't like you," I said.

"Are you quite sure about that?" said Jack, his lips still curving. The way he was looking at me made me very aware that he hadn't actually let me go: his arms were still around me, and his face was far closer than it had seemed before. Was this what he meant when he said that later things would be less boring, or was he just trying to irritate me?

I said: "Yeah, pretty sure. Are you going to help, or are you just going to keep annoying me?"

"That's hurtful," said Jack calmly, pulling me to my feet with him as he rose. Somewhere along the way he must have let me go, but it was so gradual that I didn't realise we were apart until I was trailing after him into the main room. "It's a good thing I'm inured to offence when it comes to you, Mab."

"What is it you want to tell me?" I said. I wasn't sure I was comfortable with the way the conversation was going, and I wanted to find Hatter and Hare.

"You're such a driven little person!" marvelled Jack. "Sit down. Where's the hat?"

I looked around me blankly, and found it behind the first sofa. I must have thrown it there as I came in, intent on bodily harm to Jack. I slid over the back of the sofa with it, plumping myself down on the fat black cushions, and found with some annoyance that Jack was sitting down on the same sofa. He was still sitting too close, but I didn't like to mention it because he was only studying Hatter's top hat. I didn't particularly want Jack's mocking grin directed at me again, and I was pretty sure that protesting against his closeness would be the quickest way of making that happen.

"The hat is what's important," he said, turning it over.

"Yes, you said," I said sourly. "She left it so I'd think you took Hatter and Hare."

"I hesitate to contradict you, Mab–"

"But that's what *you* said!"

"Of course, but if I know Mother Dearest it was not merely that which prompted her to leave the hat for you to find. If I know her, she had at least two or three other reasons for doing so."

"Which are?"

Jack shrugged. "I wouldn't even hazard a guess. Mother Dearest has many reasons and many schemes. The most I can tell you is that yesterday she went out early and returned before nightfall. Card sharks went out again a little later. One presumes that was in order to return the hat."

My eyes went to his face hopefully. "Then they can't be far! She didn't have time to take them anywhere else."

"She barely had time to get there and come back," said Jack. "And she certainly didn't put them in the dungeon."

"You think it has something to do with the hat as well," I said.

"It would be typical of her," shrugged Jack. "She likes being clever and tortuous about things. It would amuse her no end to know not only that she'd driven a wedge between us, but that you'd had Hatter and Hare's salvation in your hands the whole time and didn't know it."

I looked at him in silence for a moment, and then said unexpectedly: "She really did a number on you when you were a kid, didn't she?"

Jack's brows rose, but all he said was: "Let's leave my twisted little childhood out of it, shall we, Mab? It's not a very pretty story, and it reflects little credit on myself or Mother Dearest. I'll tell you all about it one day when you aren't so prickly. All I'm suggesting is that if she left that hat behind, it was with more than one purpose; so be careful about believing anything you see through it. It would probably strike her as immensely humorous to lead you on a wild goose chase."

Curiously, I asked: "Is this breaking the rules? Helping me this much, I mean?"

"It's a grey area," said Jack, after a pause. "I'm not supposed to help anyone directly. Except I'm blood bound to you, so that means I'm allowed to help you. Mother doesn't much like it but she can't really do anything about it because it's not technically breaking the rules. It's just that she expects my first loyalty to be to her."

"Oh," I said. "I was pretty sure your first loyalty was to yourself."

"Well, Miss Snip, perhaps it is," said Jack. Despite the words, he was grinning. "But she expects at least second loyalty."

"So you can help without breaking the rules if you help someone else in a way that helps me," I said thoughtfully.

"Exactly so."

"*When* you feel like helping me."

"Let's not get into that right now, either. You're not really very grateful, Mab."

"Well, I'm not used to you helping me," I said, after thinking about it. "And really, that's your fault."

"Of *course* it is!" said Jack, and now he was laughing. "And there's no possibility that you–"

"Oooh!" I said. "No, Jack, shut up!"

"You've never been particularly polite, but I must say that I do expect at the very least not to be told to shut up," said Jack.

"Sorry," I said: "Well, actually, no, I'm not sorry. You made me think of something."

"Mab," said Jack, very carefully setting Hatter's top hat on my knees and moving closer in the same motion; "I'm going to put my arm around you now, so please don't punch me."

"Why would I punch you?"

"I'm sure I don't know, but I had the distinct impression that you might."

"Wait, why are you putting your arm around me?"

"It seemed like a good idea at the time," sighed Jack, sliding his arm around my shoulders just the same. "Perhaps I'm expressing my appreciation for both your sharp tongue and wit."

"Oh. I thought you were just trying to be annoying."

"Darling Mab," said Jack coldly. "You're so good for my self-esteem!"

He didn't remove his arm, however, and I cautiously let myself relax. Jack always had been odd and hard to fathom in his reactions: I had never been sure whether he hated me, tolerated me, or really quite liked me.

"I suppose it's all right," I said.

Jack laughed at that: really laughed. Then he said: "What is this idea of yours?"

"It's what Hatter said his hat was: possibilities and probabilities. I think maybe she—well, it sounds stupid, but I think maybe she used his hat to trap them in a possible future. Or maybe a past that was probable but didn't happen. I've seen her change things in the mirrors, and if she had Hatter's hat—and knew what it could do—I think she might have been able to do it."

"That sounds just like Mother Dearest," said Jack, nodding. "Can you find out?"

"Don't know," I said. "I don't even know if it's possible—or if she did it."

"Well, if she brought them back here, they'd still be some-where about the castle and I would have noticed."

"Unless she expected me to come to you. She might have hidden them from you."

"I don't think she expected you to come to me, quite honest-ly," said Jack. "As a matter of fact, I wasn't expecting you to come to me again. Why did you?"

"I was angry," I said. That wasn't quite it, though: there was more to it. Slowly, I said: "I think I wanted you to tell me it wasn't true."

"Do you know, I think that's the closest you've ever come to giving me a compliment," said Jack. I opened my mouth to reply, but he said hastily: "Mab, if the next thing out of your mouth is an insult, I'll—I'll–"

"You'll what? Tell your mu–"

"No!" said Jack. "I'll make perishing sure you can't use your lips to say anything else by kissing you!"

I gazed up at him with my mouth open for a dumbstruck moment. What was he playing at *now*? At last I said: "You usually make a lot more sense."

"I really can't tell if you're deliberately provoking me or if you just want the chance to hit me," said Jack. "Never mind—look, supposing you're right about the hat. What can you do about it?"

"Don't know," I said again. I didn't even know if I *could* do something about it. But if I was the Queen, with her powers and her resources, I would have put Hatter and Hare into a possible future or past. The odds against anyone except Hatter being able to fix something like that were very high.

"I'm sure you'll think of something," said Jack. "You seem to see things differently. No, it's more than that: you seem to make other people see things differently. I'm still not sure if that's a gift or a curse."

I sucked in a breath between my teeth, feeling a puzzle piece click into place. I wasn't sure whether or not Jack meant to give me the answer—so hard to tell what was truth and what was illusion with Jack!—but he certainly had given me the answer. I'm not exactly sure why I did it (that was probably his fault, too) but I said: "You're very clever today, Jack," and kissed his cheek.

Then I slid down onto the floor with the hat, which made

Jack protest: "What are you doing, Mab? Come back up here at once!"

"Can't," I said. "I'm Seeing things differently."

The Queen used mirrors, so as a precaution I used the ripply bit at the top of the hat; the piece I had always thought of as a tiny, sideways pond. I wanted to make sure I had as little as possible of her influencing me, and I *was* better with ripples than with flat reflections, after all. It was just a matter of deciding whether she would have gone for past or future, and even that wasn't so hard. The Queen had a predilection for future and not much affinity for the past, if Jack was to be believed; but despite that, the easiest thing in the world for her would have been to make Hatter and Hare themselves look at things differently. For example, if she had encouraged Hare to think about a time before his front paw was cut off, it would have been possible—if not exactly easy—to trap them in a reflection of that. Hatter without his hat wouldn't have had a hope of defending himself. It was just a theory, of course, but I thought it was a good one. I looked into the ripples, changing my focus to what was already past, and what could have gone differently; and before long I saw them. Hatter and Hare at the tea table; Hatter with the most enormous cup of tea I had ever seen, and Hatter with both his paws. I saw myself pop out of a teapot in some surprise, but of course I had been there that day! This time when the Queen's carriage began to approach, however, Hatter and Hare bolted for a hidden passage beneath the tea-table, the teapot with me in it clutched in Hatter's arms. It was more of a hole than a passage, but when they dropped through it they seemed to float rather than fall; and when at last their feet touched the bottom of the shaft, the whole scene went back to the beginning. It was looped, playing again and again, a minute-long clip in Underland colours.

"Hey!" I said. "Wake up, you two! It's not real!"

Jack said something in my ear but I was focused on the hat and it didn't make sense, so I ignored it. Hatter and Hare were still proceeding in the same loop, but they looked puzzled.

"Hey!" I said again. They leaped into the hole beneath the tea-table despite my voice, and appeared at the beginning again. This time they looked suspicious and a little bit worried. At last Hatter patted his head, and finding nothing on it but hair, rather frantically began to look around. I said "Hey!" a third time, and I thought that Hare's ears pricked up slightly.

"You're not listening to me!" I said to his twitching ears. "The Queen made you think of a way that you could keep your paw. Now you're trapped in a loop of past Could-Have-Been."

"HATTER," said Hare; "I DON'T FEEL QUITE ALL THERE."

Hatter fixed an intent look on him and said: "No more do I. I'm shorter than usual, I'm sure of it."

"WHERE'S YOUR HAT?"

"Well, where's your paw?" instantly replied Hatter, and I saw with a *frisson* of excitement that Hare's paw was very slowly vanishing. It was working!

Hare said sadly: "I knew it was too good to be true. She's been playing tricks again, Hatter."

"Trick's on her," said Hatter. "That was never your best paw. I suppose we'd better jump again."

"*Don't* jump!" I said indignantly. "You'll only go back to the beginning again!"

"PISH," said Hare, almost as if he'd heard me. "AFTER YOU, HATTER."

And they jumped.

"YOW!" said Hare, suddenly present, his breath warm on my face. "HATTER, WE'RE BACK. BACK TO FRONT. AM I ME OR AM I YOU?"

"Who do you feel like?" said Hatter, just as delightfully

present. "Wait, you can't feel with that paw, you haven't got it. Try feeling with the other one."

I smiled gladly at them, and as I did so something chattered sharply behind me. The hairs stood up on the back of my neck, but before I could move sharp, clawed hands seized me from behind, digging into my flesh. There were card sharks everywhere—where had they come from?—another four pouncing on Hatter and Hare. Jack was standing by the sofa as if he had just leapt to his feet, and the Queen stood framed by the doorway, her skirts blood red and almost too wide to fit through.

I looked furiously at Jack but he said swiftly: "I didn't, Mab!"

"Jack, I'm disappointed in you, I really am!" said the Queen. "Fraternizing with your fiancée is one thing: consorting with this sort of scaff and raff is quite another!"

"SCAFF AND RAFF, MADAM?" bawled Hare at the top of his lungs. "WE ARE THE ARISTOCRATS, MADAM, THE BLUE BLO–" He stopped, his eyes bulging and his long nose twitching, and continued with a far greater amount of decorum: "Our apologies, ma'am. We are quite out of blue blood, but if you would care for a little of the red, we should be happy to oblige."

The Queen flicked him a look of disgust and turned her eyes on me, heavy-lidded with satisfaction. "As for you, little puddle-jumper," she said: "I'm glad to see that you're as predictable as ever. It's really much easier to plan on your arrival if I take the precaution of capturing your friends."

"Like dissecting frogs," I said. "Tweaking nerves and making the leg kick."

"Indeed."

"Why not just send a card?"

"Would you have come?"

"Not for you."

"I would *really* caution about being so rude when you have

ten fingers to spare," said the Queen gently. "The rabble wouldn't care to see your little face ruined, but I doubt they'd notice a finger or two."

I met Jack's eyes and found nothing comforting there. He was white and narrow-lipped. I curled my fingers into my palms, feeling the nails press in, and said: "Why am I here?"

"The time has come," she said. "You're a distraction when present and a figurehead when absent, so it seems wise to begin moulding you as befits the prince's fiancée. You will remain at the Heart Castle until Jack's twenty-fifth birthday–"

"I don't think so," I said.

The Queen's mouth remained open for just an instant, a plump red 'o'. I don't think she'd expected me to make a peep after the threat to remove a few of my fingers. Then her lips pressed together in a squashed little *moue*. "Number Four, hold out the girl's hand."

I fought, of course, but I wasn't anything like strong enough to stop my hand being forced out in front of me. The Queen rustled closer, her knife chiming lightly against the silver back of the mirror that always hung within the folds of her skirts. I was almost certain she did it on purpose, and said a mental farewell to one or two of my fingers, hoping it wouldn't hurt too much.

Jack, smoothing his tie, said: "Mother. You *know* I don't care for mutilation."

His stride was unhurried but he kept pace with her just the same. He was being very carefully slow. The Queen didn't seem to hear him, but when she lifted the blade it was only to tap it lightly against my knuckles.

"You're a very fortunate girl," she said. "Jack has his mother's sensibilities: he hates the ugly and ill-formed. I don't feel that it's appropriate to leave you unpunished, however. Which of your friends shall die for your insolence?"

"What do you want?" I said quietly. Neither Hatter nor Hare would die because of me if I could help it. "You want me to go down on my knees? I will."

"I want to punish you. Your bended knee helps me not at all." She pointed at Hare with the tip of her blade, and smiled. "This one, I think."

I gave a strangled cry, straining against the grip of the card sharks: then Jack, turning elegantly on his pointy-toed shoes, was between Hare and the Queen. Not beside, or nearby, but solidly in between them.

"Dear me!" said the Queen. She sounded amused. "Are you going to stop me, my dear? Do remember yourself, and do remember the rules before you do anything...*hasty*."

Jack met her eyes, and I thought for a bright, kindling moment that he was going to take the dagger from her. The card sharks that weren't gripping my arms were engaged in trying to hold Hatter and Hare down: they fought with the strength of madness, and the card sharks had no attention to spare for any peril in which the Queen might stand. She herself looked down at Jack in an indulgent, amused sort of way, unaware or perhaps unbelieving of her danger. The smile that had blossomed on my face died in the bud as Jack held her gaze for a fraction of a moment longer and then, looking away, stepped aside and left Hare to her mercies.

I saw the Queen's knife glitter but I thought it was the flash of light on her dangling mirror, and I didn't realise what was happening until she plunged it twice into Hare's neck. I barely had time to scream before it was over, scarlet arcs of blood flying in bright relief against the black-and-white room. I felt a wet warmth on my face that wasn't salt tears, and my fingers lost all feeling as I strained against the card sharks' grip on my arms, my breath panting loud in my ears. It could have been a gothic tableau: the Queen of Hearts, her blade naked and dripping with Hare's blood, standing over his prone body. The card sharks, teeth chattering in enjoyment. Hatter howling, as mad as I'd ever seen him. And Jack, frozen white with blood on his face and a stunned look to his eyes.

I saw the reflection of it all in the Queen's knife, awash with blood; and I said, savagely: "No."

Her gaze fell so, so, slowly, a cold understanding in her eyes, but I was already Seeing Underland differently in the bloody blade; and in that bloody blade I froze the present *Is* and dragged it back to the past *Was*. I focused on Hatter and Hare—and almost accidentally on myself and Jack—freezing the card sharks and the Queen in the other *Is* that was now *May Be*. On the carpet Hare inhaled a free breath and leapt to his paws with a giant kick of his back legs, sending his crutch flying. There was somehow still blood all over his fur, but the wound was gone. Hatter, who was chattering away to himself with a wild look in his purple eyes, looked around at the others and snatched his hat back from the frozen Number Seven.

"This is a pretty Was," he said, quite calmly. "Oughtn't you to put it back where you got it from? I'd hate to break it."

"Mab," said Jack, very quietly: "What have you done?"

"I'm not putting it back," I told Hatter, ignoring Jack with as much iciness as if he was frozen along with his mother. "This isn't *Was*, it's *Is*."

He looked around at the new present, poking at it with those purple eyes; and he must have been satisfied, because he said: "A perfect fit! A delightful job of hattery."

"Maybe not," I said. I had thought it was my imagination, but the Queen and the card sharks were still moving. They were moving almost too slowly to be seen, but I was pretty sure that they were getting quicker. They were slowly being drawn back to the new Is from what was now Might-Have-Been. "We'd better go while they're still too slow to catch us. I can take us all through the bathtub if you like."

"One is too cultured to travel by bathtub," said Hare, with a fierce glare. I took this to be a thank you for saving his life and hugged him, which seemed to confuse—though it also seemed to please—him. He made vague patting motions in the air above my head, and said, looking perplexed: "One travels via mirror, madam. Your ears are still too big."

"You can use Jack's dressing mirrors," I said, giving the Hare one last squeeze before I let him go.

"Not coming to tea?" asked the Hatter; and though his face was sad, it was also understanding. "We've got room."

"Not this time," I said quietly. It had occurred to me that the further I was from Underland, the safer Hatter and Hare would be. Whatever the Queen was planning for me, and for Underland, she couldn't do it if I wasn't there. The rebellion would simply have to do or die on its own. "Maybe in another *Then*."

I hugged him, too; as if I'd never again get the chance. I probably wouldn't. Unlike Hare, he hugged me back with fervour, spinning me in a dizzy circle. When he set me down at last, there was something on my head. I couldn't see what it was, but when I put up careful hands up to feel what it was, I found that I was wearing a small, shallow-crowned bowler with a curly brim.

"A delightful job of hattery," said the Hatter again, and followed Hare into Jack's dressing room. I didn't follow them. I stayed where I was, waiting for who knows what while the Queen and her card sharks grew steadily faster.

Someone touched my arm, and I flinched. It was Jack.

"Get off me," I said. He still had Hare's blood on his face, which was ridiculous. Hare's blood was all back inside him.

"I didn't—I didn't mean–" He seemed to pull himself together with an effort, and said lightly: "Is that any way to speak to your fiancé? The one who just helped you to find your friends, by the way?"

I looked at him in cold dislike. "Help? Is that what you call it?"

"We all have our strengths and weaknesses," he shrugged. "Perhaps you've heard the phrase *All's well that ends well*?"

He reached for me with one hand—I wasn't sure whether he was trying to wipe away the blood I could feel slowly trickling down my own face, or simply trying to comfort me—and I flinched away again.

"Get off, Jack. I don't like you and I'm not marrying you. I'm not even coming back to Underland."

"Mab, don't be like that," he said, smiling. He even took another step toward me. "There's nothing we can do about it. We might as well get along."

"*Don't* touch me!"

"Mab–"

"You stood there."

"*Mab–*"

"You stood there and let her kill him."

"Those are the rules," said Jack. He gestured at the rich room around us with one blood-splashed hand, looking past his mother. "I don't interfere, and she doesn't get rid of all this."

I gazed at him, my mouth slightly open. There was a part of me that had assumed maybe Jack was just too frightened to speak out, that maybe the Queen would cut off his hand like she had with Hare, or his finger, like the painter. It had never occurred to me that he was simply unwilling to lose his rich lifestyle.

"Believe it or not," said Jack, without quite looking at me; "I'm really not the best candidate for reduced circumstances."

"You're not the best *candidate*–"

"Wool, for instance. Absolutely dreadful for my skin."

"I actually forgot for a while," I said furiously.

"What did you forget, Mab?" asked Jack. His eyes were glittering, but he was still smiling with his face white below the crimson blood. "Oh yes, if I recall correctly, I'm a *dirtbag*. Let's be honest now: can you picture me in a hovel? Or perhaps you'd like me to live in the forest like the half-wit knight and your two mad little friends?"

"I don't care *where* you live! If it comes to that, I don't care if you die!"

"I'm very well aware of the extent of your unconcern, thank you very much!" said Jack, and this time the smile had completely vanished. There was a cold satisfaction in me for that. "You've made your feelings very clear! It doesn't change the fact that we're bound, however, and no matter how far you run or how much you squirm, there's really nothing you can do about it."

"You're always saying there's nothing you can do!" I flashed. "That's rubbish! There's lots you can do; you just won't do it because you're a coward! I meant what I said. I'm going away and I'm not coming back."

"You can't get away from me," said Jack, shrugging. I found his sudden return to calmness a little frightening.

"What are you going to do, send card sharks after me?"

"Card—of course I'm not going to send card sharks after you! Really, Mab! I think you deliberately misunderstand me."

"Yeah, well that's the only thing that'll bring me back," I told him grimly. He wasn't angry but he wasn't quite calm, either. There was a kind of brittle madness about him that I didn't recognise, and I didn't want to think how much of it had to do with the whiteness of his face or the way his nostrils were flaring. Jack didn't deserve to have human feelings. Not when he'd let Hare die without lifting a finger to help. "You can keep your pretty room and your pretty clothes—and your expensive little presents, if it comes to that! They cost too much."

That brilliant smile was back on Jack's face, bright, light and entirely reflective. "Are you sure that you're not simply furious with yourself because you egged Mother on to kill Hare? Care for one's appearance is not a character flaw, my darling. I couldn't possibly manage if I had to look after myself."

I gazed up at his face for far too long, trying to think what to say. In the end, all that seemed appropriate was a disgusted: "Ugh." I wheeled about, striding for the bathroom and my passage home.

Behind me there was a flurry of movement, and Jack's voice said, sharp and hasty: "I didn't mean it, Mab! I didn't mean any of it!"

I didn't stay to hear any more, but as I sank into the place between there and here for what I knew must be the last time, I thought I heard his voice say: "Mab! *Mab, I'm sorry!*"

12

———

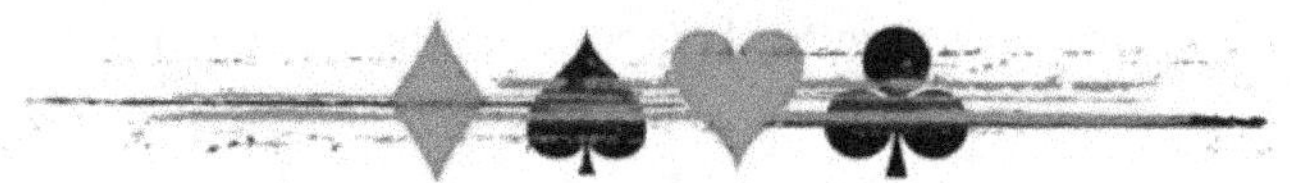

I saw her in the local Woolworths that night: the Queen, returned to life and movement, a burning anger in her eyes. I'd just opened the glass freezer door to get my six pack of frozen dagwood dogs, and when I closed it again, she was staring right at me, her eyes pale with fury. I froze, unable to look away, and the babble of the noisy store sank to a murmur around me until all I could hear was her voice.

"I have borne with your constant interference and irritation because it suited my purpose," she said. "But the nuisance you create has begun to outweigh your usefulness. Be very careful that I don't change my mind about you."

"You can change whatever you want," I said—in some bitterness, because hadn't she proved that she really *could* change whatever she wanted to? "I never asked to be dragged to Underland, and I definitely don't want to marry your son!"

"Believe me," said the Queen; "One way or another, kicking or screaming, you will return. And you *will* marry my son. I merely ask that in the meantime, you refrain from making more of a nuisance of yourself than you already have. Hare is not the first to die, and he won't be the last if you cannot control your whims."

"I've got nothing to do with it," I said, sharp and firm. "You won't see me again. Don't bother to look for me."

I turned on my heel and walked away while she was still spoke, ignoring the wary looks from other customers and the sound of her fury alike. There was no going back. Not for me, not for her. Underland had its champions, and it was safer for my friends if I wasn't one of them.

13

There was a card beneath the door of my flat a week after I got back. The cards were usually on my pillow when I woke, and it occurred to me that Jack was giving me a little space. That was worrying, because Jack didn't do things without a reason. I didn't trust it for a sign of good faith. Why couldn't he just leave me alone? I didn't want a part of him; and I almost thought that I didn't want a part of Underland any more, either. I threw the card in my bin and went around the flat making sure that every reflective surface was fully covered. The next day I set out to find a new flat.

The new flat gave me a brief respite, but when I started work at the library two weeks later and opened the returns flap in the front door, the first thing I saw was a pair of black-flecked eyes.

"Hello darling," said Jack.

I shut the flap in his face, but he was still there when I had to open the doors to the public. He smoothly passed both the doors and my scowl, and made a game of prowling the library while I tried alternately to keep my eye on him and ignore him completely. Much to my annoyance, he also made a game of turning up behind me for the pleasure of murmuring in my ear and making me jump.

"Jack, if you do that just *once* more, I'm going to punch you!" I said at last, in a low growl.

"Mab! I'm surprised at you! And in a library, too!"

I gave him the brittle smile that had already frightened off many a book vandal, and said: "The librarians don't care if I punch people, so long as I do it quietly."

"You've been ignoring my cards."

"Yes, and I'm going to keep ignoring them. Look, the head librarian is watching us: you're going to get me fired. Go away."

Jack sent a lazy, arrogant look in the head librarian's direction. "Don't worry, I can manage her."

"Also, I don't like you. *Go away.*"

"Is that any way to speak to your–"

I seized him by the front of his collar and shoved him into the less-travelled audiobook corner, rattling tapes in their cases.

"You are *not* my fiancé."

Jack, his hands spread wide, innocently said: "Now, Mab, if you wanted to get me by myself in a quiet corner, all you had to do is ask."

"What do you want?"

"Well, there's this prickly girl who keeps running away from me. My fiancée, as a matter of fact. She covers her mirrors and refuses to answer to the cards I leave her. More importantly, she won't let me apologise."

"Go away, Jack. I'm not interested in your apologies, and I have a job to do!"

"As do I," said Jack. His hands, which had been spread wide, now slid around my waist. "It's a very important job, and it requires my apologies."

I saw the head librarian making her way forcefully toward

us, and hissed: "Jack, if you don't let me go *right now,* you're going to be very sorry!"

"I'm certain I'll be much sorrier if I do," said Jack, and pulled me further into the audiobooks with him.

When the head librarian turned the corner Jack was trying to kiss me and I was trying to stop him. I'm not sure who was the most annoyed to be interrupted: me, as I lost the chance to follow through with my threat to punch him; or Jack, who had just managed to pin my arms to my sides. Jack was completely capable of charming the head librarian, but when he left I proved incapable of following his example and was given notice. It didn't really matter, of course: if Jack could find me, so could the Queen and her card sharks. I had to move again.

The next week I found a basement flat that had no windows, in the oldest, grubbiest part of the city. The windows that *were* nearby were broken, and the rent was manageable. I covered the bathroom mirror and learned to do my hair by feel.

And I tried to forget.

14

———

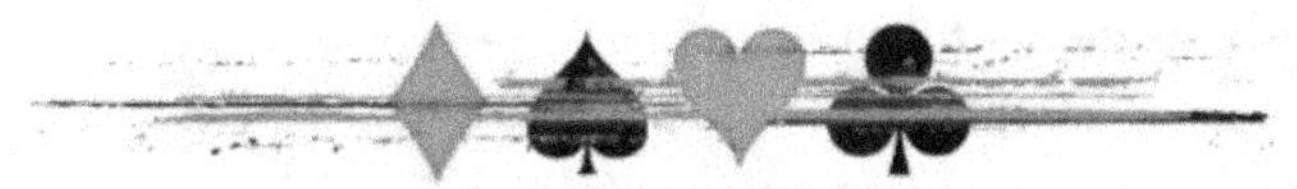

A year passed: a year of quietness and freedom from Underland and its people. And if life and reality felt a little flat, well, that was only to be expected. Australia just wasn't as colourful or as full of life as Underland. I was careful, but the feeling of danger can't be sustained over the course of a year when there's nothing to feed it, and perhaps I wasn't careful enough.

It started the way it usually starts: with a card. It was on my pillow that morning when I woke, its red pips showing up clearly against the whiteness of the pillow-slip. The Jack of Hearts. I knew exactly who'd left it, and what would be on the back of it; but I turned it over anyway. It had been such a long time since I'd seen one. It said: *You're invited. It's a very important date. Don't be late.* I gave a soft sniff of laughter: as if I'd go anywhere Jack invited me! I had a date tonight, anyway. I'd even bought a new dress for it; a green, airy thing that almost looked like a flapper-dress but was too short to really be one. It wasn't warm enough for the night, but I wore stockings by way of compromise, and a warm little hat that made the '20s effect even more pronounced. I even wore high-heels, plain black mary-janes that strapped across my foot and ankle, and I lightly swung a long, slender-handled parasol between my fingers. The parasol wasn't new: I'd found it in the streets by someone's rubbish. It was small and purposely raggedy, in faded butterfly colours that delighted me, and I'd exulted in my find for a full week afterwards. It was no practical use, of course, but at a pinch it *might* keep off a few snowflakes. I probably shouldn't have twitched aside the towel I kept over the bathroom mirror, but it had been so long, and I wanted to see how I looked. It was my first real date, and I was nervous. Besides, I hadn't seen a sight or reflection of the Queen since last year. I hoped, somewhat worriedly, that she'd given up.

Considering the card, it might have been wiser to wear flat shoes. Or to think about moving apartments again, if it came to that. I didn't do either: I set out at 6.30 exactly, my hat set at a jaunty angle, and carefully pranced down the street in my heels. I didn't have far to walk, and although there was still snow on the ground and puddles in the street, it seemed safe enough. I was only halfway down Harris Street by the time I realised my mistake. One card shark segued from beside the usual homeless man as I passed, and another broke free from the darkened doorway of the library. I saw them both in the window reflections, and caught the suggestion of another two or three behind *them*. I knew better than to look around, but I did begin to walk a little faster. There was no safety in lights and company: card sharks would push through the crowd and drag me off by force without thinking twice.

I found myself all but running down Harris Street, trying to avoid the worst of the slurry and not quite sure of where I was going except that I needed to shake the card sharks before I could sneak back home. I entered Harris Park at a good trot, throwing a swift look around. There were two policemen at the far end, where the park dipped into a few walking trails that were convoluted enough to hide me from the sharks while I found my way safely home. They were talking to a woman in a red business suit who seemed to be pointing in my direction—silly to think that, but it really did look like it—and they would be absolutely no help. If anything, they would only provide a few moments' distraction for the card sharks. That the distraction would consist of two policemen being eaten alive and kicking was a fact of which I was very much aware. I desperately wanted to get away, but I didn't think I could face the idea of sacrificing two policemen in my escape.

I began to edge slightly to my left, making for a gap in the trees, and came up against a series of deep puddles straight ahead that made me veer even more sharply to the left. There was no way I was going to step through a puddle. Someone was trying to make very sure I ended up in Underland, and that could only mean something very bad was about to happen. The policemen had begun a gentle sort of a trot uphill toward me, and I resigned myself to the path I'd taken. There were too many puddles behind me to run that way, anyway. I could see a road up ahead: if I was lucky, there would also be a street in which to lose myself once I was out of the soft grass.

The soles of my shoes slapped against wet grass in a frantic, soggy series of squishes. The road was in my sight, and I hurried to reach it, conscious of the card sharks quickly gaining on me. I came upon it too suddenly, a sudden drop from grass to curb, and from curb to water-logged road, and for a moment I teetered on the edge of the grassy curb with frantically wind-milling arms. Cold panic came to my rescue: I fiercely stabbed at the grass with the point of my parasol and caught myself just in time. My reflection in the shallow water below was open-mouthed and wide-eyed. I'd almost fallen in. Back into Underland. Back into madness. Back into danger.

And if I wasn't very careful, I could still end up in Underland: the puddle was *massive.* Icy at the edges, snowy all around, and impinging on the road to fully half way. I'd jumped bigger, but never in heeled shoes, and *never* in the snow. There was a good chance I'd break my ankle—or worse, my neck—if I made it across. On the other hand, broken ankle or not, at least I wouldn't be in Underland.

A wild look over my shoulder showed only danger: card sharks to my left; massive, impassable sheets of water behind me; police sprinting up the hill from the right. I had to jump. The puddle in the gutter was big, but it was smaller than the shallow oceans behind me. I threw another look around, my breath misting the air, and leaped.

I saw the pale golden flash of winter sun on slurried water, felt the bite of the wind on my cheeks. My parasol snatched at the air behind me, slowing me, but I saw my right foot splash down safely in snowy slurry. I slipped, and someone caught me tightly around the waist, warm and strong. I grabbed desperately for his waist with my free hand, sequins scratching against red velvet.

Red velvet. A splashing of slurry. A *splashing.*

Oh no.

"Got you!" said Jack.

"Hope I stood on your toe," I panted, conscious that my skirt was less than decent and that I was showing at least one row of lace from my lace undershorts.

"You did," Jack said. "I didn't think heels were your style, Mab. I must say, I really approve. *What* a delightful dress!"

"What do you want?"

"Far too nice to wear out for a casual stroll, and those stockings—you're on a date!"

"What do you want, Jack?"

"I want to know who you're dating, for starters! You're engaged to me!"

"I'm *not* engaged to you," I said. "I was kidnapped by your mad-as-a-loon mother when I was three and she made us trade drops of blood. I had nothing to do with it."

"I see you liked the birthday present I sent you," he said, shrugging off the question for later. And it *would* come up later. It always did, with Jack. He just liked to make sure that he held all the aces when he brought it back up.

"What birthday—oh." The parasol. I should have realised. It was far too beautiful for someone to simply leave in the street. And it had matched the dress so perfectly. Suspiciously, I added: "Did you know what I was going to wear today?"

"I don't know what you're talking about. Why didn't you come when I sent you the card?"

"I didn't want to be stuck in Underland again. You sent card sharks after me!"

Jack's brows snapped together. "*Card sharks?* No."

"Then who—" I remembered the woman in the red suit, pointing the policemen in my direction. I said grimly: "Oh."

"Mother Dearest, I presume," said Jack, nodding. He still looked worried. "I was hoping she wouldn't find out."

I stared at him even more suspiciously. "Find out what? What have you done?"

Was it my imagination, or did he look guilty? "I may or may not have incited rebellion."

"You *what*?"

"I didn't mean to," he said, looking away.

"What do you mean you didn't mean to?"

"It all happened so suddenly! There were vigilantes, and people dying, and–"

My mouth must have dropped open at some stage, because he looked at me and away again quickly, and added: "Do shut your mouth, Mab. You'll catch flies."

"There aren't any flies in Underland. Do you mean to say

that you've done something noble for the first time in your spoiled little life?"

"I wouldn't call it noble exactly. It was more of an accident."

"Leaving a bloody handprint on the door?"

"You still remember that, do you? No, that was in the rules. This is against the rules."

"Is Hatter safe? What about Hare?"

"Who do you think suggested I send for you? They think you might be able to help, and I get the impression they think you'll be safer here."

I couldn't help the glad smile that warmed my face, but I also couldn't help asking: "Is that why the Queen wants me as well?"

"I imagine so," said Jack. He looked actually tired—aristocratically, nobly tired, of course, but tired just the same. "The timing is simply too coincidental. It could have something to do with our blood bond, though, for all I know. She's tricky like that."

"You said that was just an old ceremony!"

Jack pinched the bridge of his nose. "Obviously I need sleep. I'm beginning to lose track of my lies."

"You could just try *not* lying," I said flatly.

"Don't be ridiculous, Mab. There's nothing more dangerous than the truth. I'm not going to go bandying it about, willy-nilly."

"This is why you don't have any friends."

"I don't have any friends because my mother likes playing with little warm things, particularly the male ones. It has nothing to do with my veracity."

"Or your habit of speaking like you just swallowed a dictionary, I suppose?"

"*Darling* Mab," said Jack, smiling coldly. "Always so spiky and morose. Tell me again why your foster homes never kept you for longer than a few months? Ow! *Must* you always resort to violence?"

"It's part of my rules," I said. "I'm surprised you didn't know. Being engaged and everything. Wait, how did you know I'd come ho—back exactly *here*, anyway?"

"I didn't," said Jack. "That was also one of your mad little friends: the Hatter sent me a message yesterday. I didn't even know you were coming back until then. And if it comes to that, I'd like to know why you've been ignoring my card again. It's horribly rude of you."

"You break into my flats and leave things on my pillow. That's creepy."

"I prefer to think of it as polite attention. In case you've forgotten, we're to be married this year."

"Oh yes! That reminds me!" I said, firmly. "Don't change the subject again: you've been lying to me about that, too!"

"That injures me, Mab."

"And so will my fist, if you don't start talking. The blooding ceremony when I was a kid—that really does mean something, doesn't it? More than just your mad mother deciding that we're to be married."

"I didn't exactly lie," said Jack. "It *is* an old ceremony. It's just a bit more ah, official than I may have led you to believe. And a lot more binding when we're in the same world."

"What if I go back to my own world?"

"That would be a pity," said Jack. "You'd miss all the action. Oh, and your knightly friend could die."

"Sir Blanc! What's wrong with Sir Blanc?"

"He's a lot cleverer than he used to be, but not quite as wise," said Jack. "Anyone with any sense would have hidden himself away after he got his wits back. Instead, it seems that Sir Blanc has been working with your other friends for the last few years, travelling all over Underland to meddle with reflections he really shouldn't have been meddling with. Mother Dearest didn't realise in time that they'd been tampered with and before she knew it there was an attack on the Heart Castle...which I may or may not have assisted."

"Opened the doors for them, did you?"

"Something like that," Jack said.

"It's not like you to be modest," I remarked.

"Oh, I haven't yet gotten to the part where I fought off four card sharks and rescued a beautiful maiden."

I frowned. "Rescued a–"

"Relax, darling," said Jack, with a glittering smile, "That's you. I wouldn't dream of rescuing any other damsels. You've no need to be jealous."

"Why would I be jealous?" I began, and then, goaded, "Oh, never mind that! *Where* is Sir Blanc, and *what* went wrong?"

Jack was still smiling, but he said: "I take it you remember Mother's Mirror Hall?"

My eyes widened. "Of course I do! Sir Blanc sneaked into the *Mirror Hall*?"

"Some months ago, apparently: he's been working hard at hiding certain important details from Mother. He was trying to influence the battle from within the Hall when she caught sight of him. She sent card sharks in and sealed it so that no one can get out. No one else has dared to try and go in after her."

"So he's still stuck in there?"

"And running out of food, or so I'm told. Mother's in there, too. I had an idea that she thought I was dead, but if she went to the trouble of finding you and took the time to send card sharks after you, no doubt she knows that I helped the rebellion."

"You think she wants to kill me in revenge?"

"I'd say yes, but it seems too simplistic for her. She's more likely to want you as leverage over me. You know, *stop rioting and rebelling or I'll kill your fiancée.*"

"But if she's stuck in the Mirror Hall, what can she—oh."

Jack nodded grimly. "Exactly. She's trying to change Underland in the reflections. We've already lost more than a few of our leaders. Hatter and Hare thought that if you were in Underland she'd have a bit of a harder time changing things. *I* thought that we could go in after her."

"We?"

"Well, I'm coming with you, obviously."

"When did you get so brave?"

"I'm not," said Jack. "I'm still a coward. If we run into Mother Dearest while we're in the Mirror Hall, I'll run and leave you to your fate."

"Thanks," I said, grinning. "Where are Hatter and Hare? Are you taking me to them? Are they coming too?"

"Well, that's the thing," said Jack. "They haven't exactly approved the mission."

"But you said–"

"You shouldn't listen to what I say: I keep forgetting that I don't have to lie anymore." Jack paused, frowning, and explained: "They wanted you here. They don't necessarily want you *there*."

"Oh," I said. Hatter and Hare were still acting as though I was a child. Allowed to do small, helpful things, but to be kept away from danger. "Well, we'd better not tell them, then. Are you sure you want to come with me?"

"I knew I could count on you to do exactly what you were told not to do," said Jack. "Mab, you are delightfully predictable. Can you take us to the Mirror Hall without attracting Mother's attention?"

"No," I said. "She'll know as soon as we get there. Do you still want to come with me?"

"Yes," he said. "She won't kill me."

"Are you sure?"

Jack said: "Yes. Yes of course," but there was enough of a pause between the words to make me sure that he didn't believe it himself. "Look, Mab, can we get on with it? I'll change my mind if I have to stand here thinking about it much longer."

I suppose we could have planned it better. We could have actually *made* a plan if it came to that. I don't think it would have come out any better, but maybe it would have. Who knows? The Queen, on the other hand, had certainly had time to plan, and plan she had. As soon as I stepped into the ripples with Jack, he was torn from me. I didn't realise until a moment later in the Mirror Hall that she'd been expecting us—expecting *both* of us —and that she'd sent Jack straight to one of the mirrors. There were card sharks with him, pinching and tearing and tugging at him, and they weren't gentle about tying him up to one of the Heart Castle chairs.

"There you are at last!" said the Queen. I looked around swiftly: there were so many mirrors that it was difficult to tell which Queen was the one who spoke. Jack was easier to see; he was the only Jack there. Sir Blanc was in the next mirror along, pounding furiously at the glass.

"Sorry to keep you waiting," I said. Jack, in his mirror, said something rude and pulled furiously at the ropes that tied him. The card sharks only chattered their laughter at him and leapt back into the mirror hall through his glass. "You wanted to see me?"

"You've been a festering thorn in my side since the first day I saw you," said the Queen, drawing closer. It was easier to see which one was really her, now: she was using up too much effort to reflect herself through the hall, and it was making the copies glitter as though seen through glass.

"Well, you've only got yourself to blame, haven't you?" I said. I didn't waste my energy reflecting myself. I'd need it all soon enough. "You're the one who brought me here in the first place."

She gave an impatient shrug. "Nonsense! Do you imagine that I could have kept you from Underland? No, I've seen your sort before: by hook or by crook, you weasel your way into Underland, and the results are always catastrophic. Riots, anarchy, rebellion—no, I preferred to control the narrative."

"Is that what my engagement to Jack was about? Controlling the narrative?"

"Partly that, partly common sense. I'd rather keep any of your progeny very close to me: one never knows if or when the gift will out in the children."

"And you thought that if the rest of Underland knew I was allied with the Heart family they would be less likely to fall in behind me, even if I did try to cause trouble."

"Indeed. And who knew? Perhaps you could be persuaded that the Heart way was the best way. I thought that if I could get to you early enough, you might imprint."

"I'm not the imprinting sort," I said.

"So I noticed. You should have tried. Now I'm afraid that I will have to be more convincing."

"Is that why you've got Jack tied to a chair?"

"Don't take me for a fool. I've seen you both together: you'd no more allow him to be hurt than he would allow you to be hurt."

"She obviously doesn't know how much I dislike you," I said to Jack.

"Obviously not," he agreed.

"I see you're determined to make things difficult," said the Queen. "What a shame. Card sharks! Fall in!"

Card sharks segued from the frame of Jack's mirror, numbers One through Four: all of them were chattering excitedly, and all of them had a pair of very large scissors. Jack went perfectly white and said something even ruder than before.

The Queen said: "For every minute that you defy me, one

of the sharks will cut off a piece of Jack. Lest that should fail to be convincing..." she let the sentence trail off as dozens more of the card sharks filed into the Mirror Hall, surrounding us.

I laughed, and as I did, I saw the first signs of fear in the Queen's face. "You shouldn't be laughing," she said, but she was breathing too quickly. "You should be either running or surrendering."

The card sharks flocked me, their teeth chattering in anticipation of gory pleasure, and in the mirror opposite me, Jack was tearing his arms and legs bloody by thrashing madly in his chair.

"Relax, Jack," I said. "You'll hurt yourself."

His breath hitched in his throat. "Mab–"

"What, you're worried about these things?" I looked around at the card sharks scornfully, and in the reflections, I Saw them differently. "They can't hurt me. They're nothing but a pack of cards!"

The Queen shrieked as the card sharks collapsed in a slithery, papery pack of cards around me, their pips showing hearts. She pointed one trembling finger at me and said: "You! I unmake you!"

I felt something move in the mirrors, and for a moment I saw the flash of reflection that had me never coming to Underland, never meeting Hatter and Hare, or Jack, or Sir Blanc. The Queen Saw Underland as if I had never sullied it, and at first I Saw it too. Then the mirrors seemed to stutter, and the reflection ground to a halt.

"I'm not an Underlander," I told her, feeling as though I had to gasp in relief but unwilling to show her how frightened I'd been. "You can't unmake me."

"Unmake Mabel, and you'll unmake Underland," said Sir Blanc, from his reflected prison. "Underland is made after her reflection: it shall never again be yours for the shaping. Child, you must finish this game. Unmake the Queen."

"I would think very carefully before I did that, were I you," said the Queen. She was afraid, deathly afraid, sweat dotting her white brow. I was already thinking very carefully, and she knew it. She also knew that it was quite possible I wouldn't think in the same way as she did. "You'd let Jack die? No, worse than die—you'd let Underland continue as though he'd never existed? Reflect me out of Underland, make it as though I never was, and you'll never have known Jack."

I saw the dawning of understanding in Jack's black-flecked eyes. They met mine, fear and resignation fluttering there in plain sight. He said: "G-give me a kiss before you do it, Mab."

"Don't be silly," I said. "I'm not going to kill you."

"You'd better," he said. "All things being even I'd really prefer not to cease existing, but I do think it's the only way."

"You must unmake her," urged Sir Blanc, and I found I could still think of the old, witless Sir Blanc with regret. "The boy is correct, we must seize the chance."

I turned to face Sir Blanc. "I'm sorry, Sir Blanc, but it's time for you to go." I opened his mirror to the outside world and reflected him back out, then closed it again. He would come after us as quickly as he could, but he would have a bit of a journey to get to the physical place of the Mirror Hall, and no other mirror would let him in.

"A good choice," said the Queen, smiling at me.

"Shut up," I said, stepping into Jack's mirror. "Nobody asked you."

"An interesting choice," she said. "But ultimately dangerous, don't you think? Now you're a reflection in the Mirror Hall: a rather perilous place to be."

"Oh no," I said, with one hand on Jack's shoulder. "I think you've misunderstood."

"It's all right, Mab," he said. "Unmake her. It won't end until she's gone, or never has been, or whatever mad little scenario it takes."

"You've misunderstood, too," I said, and smiled at him. "Shut up, Jack."

He gave a soft sniff of laughter and held his tongue. The Queen, on the other hand, looking at me curiously, said: "I've sealed the reflection. You won't be escaping this mirror very quickly, I'm afraid. It will give me some time to decide what to do with you. A ransom from your little friends, perhaps. Or a call to surrender. Who knows? Perhaps I shall choose to be merciful."

"You've misunderstood," I said again. "I See you, and you're just a reflection."

"I'm not a reflection," she said uneasily.

"Are you sure?" I asked. I could See it so clearly: her, caught in the reflection of the mirror's frame that had once been a frame for the mirror Jack and I were in. I had a moment's regret for what I was about to do: I would never again be able to do so much with so little effort as I did here in the Mirror Hall. And maybe that was best. The Queen had had this power, and she had misused it. "Are you *really* sure? Because I See you within the frame of a mirror, and you're only a reflection."

"I am not a reflection!" said the Queen, striding for the edge of the frame. She recoiled when she reached it, thrown back into the mirror in which I Saw her. "What have you done?"

"I told you," I said. "I told you twice. If you're not going to listen, I won't repeat myself."

Jack said, "Mab?"

"I know," I said. "I'm sorry, I have to do it."

"Do it now," he said, an edge of old madness to his black-flecked eyes. "Do it now before she finds a way out!"

"I knew I should have drowned you at birth," the Queen said

to him, with terrifying calmness. "I almost did, you know. I could have started again with a girl. I could have—I should have started with *her*. She's twice the Heart that you are, you miserable little whelp."

"You're broken," I said to her—to the mirror—to the Mirror Hall itself.

I Saw it shatter. I Saw her shatter, screaming. And I Saw the pieces falling around Jack and I in a shower of glittering glass and reflection as every last reflection died in the Mirror Hall. I ducked my head under the intermittent shower of glass and felt it sting my scalp as the Queen screamed in fractured sound and died. Glass danced at our feet and sang against the walls, and then there was a tinkling kind of silence. I cautiously raised my head and Jack shook out the glass from his hair. Most of it had missed us, but the rest of the hall was littered with shards and splinters.

I let out a shaking breath and said: "This is going to take a bit of cleaning up."

"Oh, Mab!" said Jack, with a hitch in his breath that just came short of a dry sob. "You have no idea how glad I am that you didn't kill me!"

I threw my arms around him, dizzy with relief, because it hadn't occurred to me how much it would matter if Jack was suddenly no longer in my life—cowardice, self-conceit, and all. It was easier to hug him if I sat in his lap, so I did, my face pressed into his collar. I heard him say: "As enjoyable as this is, Mab, I have to say that I feel a little at a disadvantage. If you're at liberty to embrace me I would appreciate the same freedom. I'd also like to mention the glass shard that is at present lodged in my collar."

I choked on a laugh, because it was so like Jack. "Sorry," I said, standing. "I'll untie you."

"There's no need to get off my lap," he protested. "I merely wish to have the use of my hands. I'm sure you could have untied them from there."

"You told me to kill you," I said, circling the chair to inspect the knots that tied his hands.

He craned his head to follow me and said: "Yes, and don't expect me ever to do it aga–"

I'm not sure when—or even *if*—I decided to kiss him. Maybe it was just to shut him up. I don't know. But I kissed him; and when I let go Jack said in a rather strained kind of voice: "Mab, I would really appreciate the use of my hands right now."

"I know," I said. "That's why I did *that* before I untied you."

"Untie me at once!"

"No," I said, sitting on the only clear bit of floor by his chair. "Not until you're sensible."

I did untie him at some stage. It made sense to get out of the Mirror Hall, after all, and the chair the sharks had tied him to didn't have wheels. By the time I did untie him, Jack was looking narrow-eyed and dangerous, and I wasn't quite sure if I was relieved or disappointed that he didn't repay my kiss in kind. He did hold my hand as we carefully made our way between mirror shards, but since his hands were still shaking I thought it was likely that he simply needed the comfort.

When we were outside on the steps we sat down. It seemed easier than standing to wait for Hatter and Hare, who would no doubt soon be here; and Sir Blanc, who would be here a lot more quickly. If Jack was shivering, well, so was I. I didn't object when he put his arm around me again, and this time he didn't check first to make sure I wouldn't punch him.

15

"It's your fault after all," said Jack. We were standing together in the ruins of the Heart Castle, roughly where the Queen's curio room had once been but at a considerably lower altitude. We hadn't been far apart since Hatter, Hare, and Sir Blanc retrieved us from the shattered Mirror Hall. Mostly that was because Hatter and Hare had spouted and shouted and gone slightly more mad than usual, but a small part was also Sir Blanc's insistence that I should be sent back to Australia. I didn't hold it against him: after all, he was only trying to look after me and Underland both as best he knew. And as far as he knew, I didn't belong in Underland—not really. Jack didn't share his feelings and stayed as close to me as possible, suspicious that Sir Blanc would try to send me back when no one was paying attention. Or maybe he was just afraid I'd go back on my own. Whatever the reason, we spent most of our time together. What with all the shouting and mess, however, we hadn't had much time to actually talk, and when Jack had suggested a trip to the routed Heart Castle, I agreed with a flattering swiftness.

"I was quite happy being selfish and rich, actually," he added, now. "And now look at me! Prince of a pile of ruins!"

"You're not prince of anything," I told him, grinning. "We abolished the monarchy, remember? You helped."

"Yes, and that's your fault, too. The effects of a good woman on a man, etcetera, etcetera."

"You can't expect me to believe that I'm 'the woman who changed you'!"

Jack looked distinctly rueful. "Oh, yes and no, Mab: yes and no!"

I wasn't inclined to let him get away with it. "It's a bit stereo-typical, though, isn't it? You're usually more original."

"I say *no*," said Jack evenly; "Because no matter how much I l —no matter *how* fond of you I am, if it had just been a matter of showing you that I was a better man than I am, well, I could have put on a reasonably good show. Credit me with a little intelligence, Mab! I didn't change to try and please you."

I couldn't help it. I laughed. "Prosaic of you, Jack! You're supposed to admit to all kinds of wrongs and to go down on bended knee before me!"

"If I thought that would work, I would have tried it."

"No you wouldn't," I said, still grinning. "You'd wrinkle your trousers."

"The *yes*," continued Jack, repressively; "No, do shut up, Mab! I'm baring my soul, which is a lot more important than creasing my trousers! I said *yes* because you're the one who made me see myself. At least, I saw myself through your eyes, and I didn't particularly like what I saw. Since I'm going to have to live with myself whether or not you ever marry me, I thought the best thing to do would be to change."

"Just like that?"

"Well, not exactly. It was a lot easier to decide than to *do*, so if I occasionally relapse, you'll have to forgive me."

"Oh, I will, will I?"

"Mab, I'm trying to tell you that I love you!"

The world froze around me, then kaleidoscoped. "What? Wait, *what*?"

"You can't have failed to notice it!" Jack protested. "I've been following you around like a stray puppy since last year!"

I opened and closed my mouth several times before I said: "I thought you were just being annoying! How was I supposed to know that you were in love with me?"

"I tried to kiss you multiple times," said Jack, becoming firm. "There's no excuse for you, Mab! I'd also like to point out that when a man tells you he loves you, you're supposed to reply in kind. You're not supposed to look stunned. *Or* as if you're about to run away, for that matter. It's highly insulting."

"But I don't know if I love you!" I protested. "I've never so much as gone out with another man! I've always been around you! If it comes to that, the most I can say about you is that I got used to you."

"May I remind you that *you* kissed *me*, Mab? Twice, if my memory serves me correctly."

"That's true," I said fairly. It was also true that when I'd kissed him it had been with the single, searing thought in my head that I didn't think I could have borne it if he *had* died that day. It occurred to me that I might be a little fonder of Jack than I knew. "And I do like your nose."

Jack blinked. "You like...my *nose*?"

"It's so aristocratic!" I explained. "All right, all right; maybe I'm fond of you. *Maybe.*"

"I can work with that," said Jack. "You won't expect me to dress like Hatter, will you? I really can't be expected to wear motley."

"I suppose I can put up with the pointy shoes," I said. "And now that you're not wearing red you look rather nice."

"Well, I suppose that's something," said Jack. "I ask because I'll be twenty-five in a month or two, and I'm afraid that I haven't quite impressed upon you the extent of our blood bond."

I fixed him with a glare. "What exactly does that mean?"

"I might have under-represented the influence it has while we're both in Underland."

"Jack!"

"There's nothing at all to worry about," said Jack irrepressibly. "Just make sure that you're good and in love with me by then, and it won't matter. But if you notice, by and by, that you find me irresistible, don't blame me!"

"And by irresistible you mean–"

"Exactly," nodded Jack. "Physically bound to me until we tie the knot. I'm sure it won't be as inconvenient as it sounds."

"What if I'm not—not *fond* enough of you by then?"

"Oh, don't worry," said Jack, gazing down at me with such an expression in his eyes that I couldn't look away; "I fully intend to make sure that by then you're as much in love with me as I am with you."

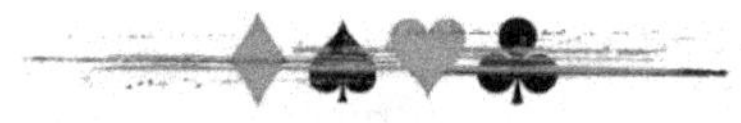

Thanks for reading! Please take a moment to write a review on your favourite storefront as a help to other readers and your friendly indie author (me)!

ABOUT THE AUTHOR

W.R. Gingell is a Tasmanian author who is definitely not getting old. She loves to rewrite fairytales with a twist or two—and a murder or three—and original fantasy where dragons, enchantresses, and other magical creatures abound. Occasionally she will also dip her toes into the waters of SciFi.

W.R. spends her time reading, drinking an inordinate amount of tea, and slouching in front of the fire to write. Like Peter Pan, she never really grew up, and is still occasionally to be found climbing trees.